THE GLASS-STAINED PATH

The Glass-Stained Path

A DARK FAIRY TALE NOVELLA
BY DREW DUNMOORE

The Glass-Stained Path
Copyright © 2021 by Beth Bandit Books LLC
All rights reserved.

First Edition

Paperback ISBN: 979-8-9860042-4-2
eBook ISBN: 979-8-9860042-5-9

Contents

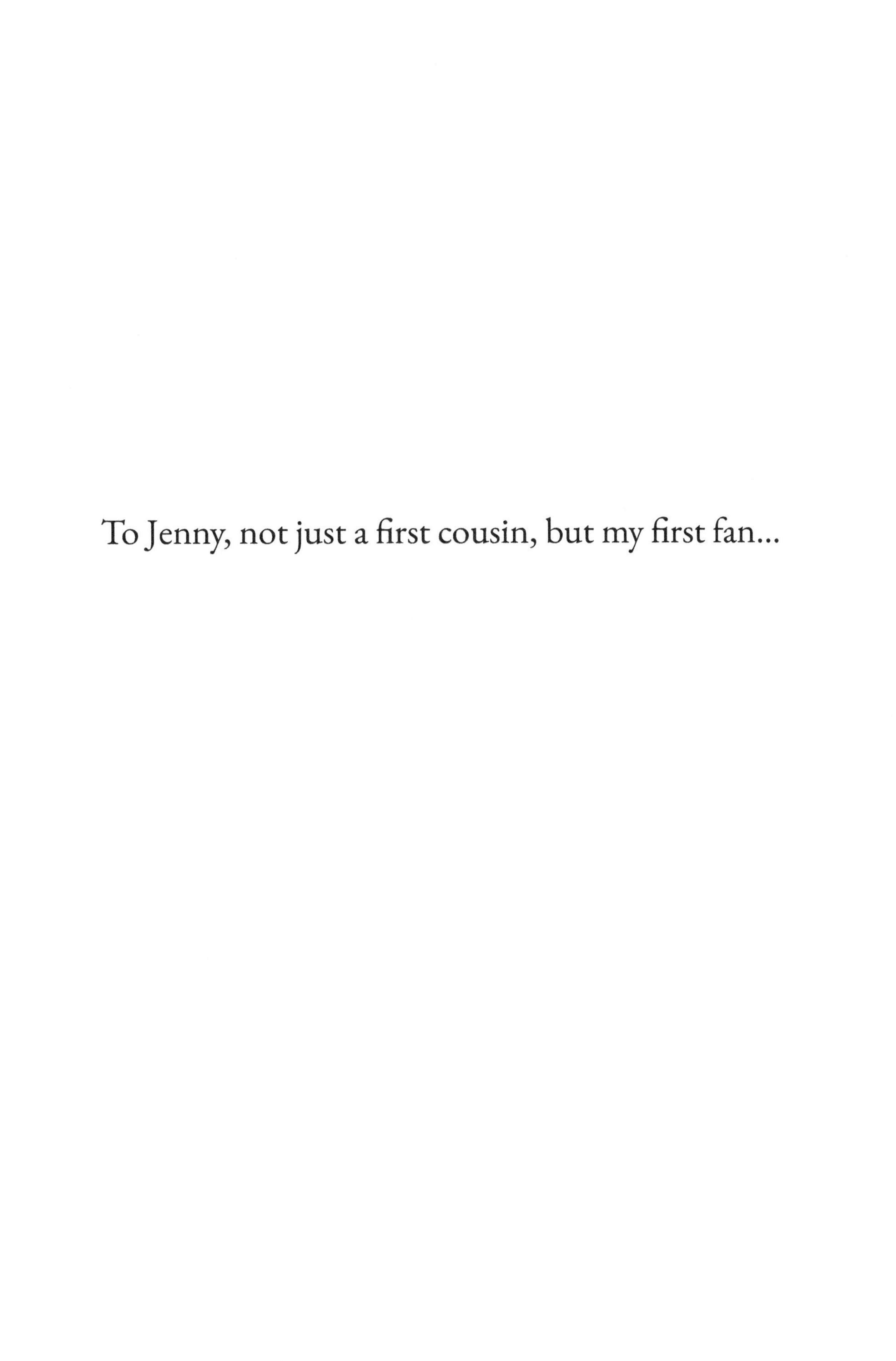

To Jenny, not just a first cousin, but my first fan...

This is a tale of good and evil, of truth and lies, but most of all, it is a tale of life and death. The lessons in this story are as old as the beginning of time for the light and the darkness walk this earth together, illuminating it and casting shadows everywhere.

In the heart of this fairy tale is the forest of the fallen, and in the forest lives the owl, the wolf, and the bear, a mighty trio.

Sinister forces reach far and wide in this land, and you might not be sure who the sinners and the saints are. Because, as it is written, Satan knows how to disguise himself as an angel of the light. The devil is a trickster, you see, and the only thing awaiting you behind his smoke screen is death. But fear not, for there is a power far greater than he, and every purpose under heaven has its season.

We begin this tale by introducing Orlawn, the owl. He's pleased to meet you and ready to accompany us down The Glass-Stained Path...

The Owl's Autumn Tutelage

THE OWL

Orlawn was the owl, and oh what a father of an owl he was!

Orlawn fathered the forest

for us.

More than the other owls, he possessed a mightier power

and in far greater caliber.

His eyes shined bright;

sunshine yellow in the night.

Orlawn's claws skimmed fast the river,

like a shooting arrow in a skillful archer's quiver.

He never missed

snatching a fish.

When he heard footsteps on the ground,

his head twisted all the way around.

His wings glided stealthily through the air

right before the mice fell prey to his snare.

Those mice

were twice as nice

when he could get one in each claw.

He got them before his sharp talons they saw.

They say his beak was made of gold,

and massive weight his steel like talons could hold.

Because his wings were the color of the trees,

you couldn't see him between the leaves.

If he flew overhead,

you were as good as dead.

This raptor was craftier

and faster

than any other raptor.

He was the master.

His perch nestled at the top of the tallest oak tree,

on the tallest mountain in the forest where he could see

everything for days and days

through the moonbeams and sunrays.

Orlawn's eyes could peer down,

beyond the rivers and streams

and into the neighboring town.

Orlawn knew it all,

and the night belonged to him in the fall.

When the autumn wind got forceful and blew around,

he took shelter in the hole of a great oak tree high above the ground.

This hole housed a whole parliament of owls,

while the wind let out its howls.

Each owl was wiser than the next,

but all knowing Orlawn to be the best.

When the parliament gathered face to face,

quite a coup took place.

You might think the wolves and bears ruled the forest because they're so large,

but the owls were in charge,

with the knowledge of the forest

singing whispers of wisdom between their feathers like a chorus.

As the saying goes, knowledge is power,

especially at the witching hour.

Orlawn met the witch many moons ago when she was but just a girl.

Her mother taught her how anything could querl.

Orlawn said to her, "You are a beautiful witch."

Great friends they were ever since.

PASHMEIRA THE WITCH AND ORLAWN THE OWL

In the beginning, there was dark and light, separated by day and night. When a host of angels fell from the heavens, the dark roamed amongst the light, like a lion looking for a fight. Every kind of creature imaginable inhabited the land, and the seasons were separated by God's hand. Along came man and woman. They were told not to be shy but to be fruitful and multiply.

No one took the multiplying more seriously than King Kurlbach. Much more than one hundred years ago, during the early years of King Kurlbach's reign, he exiled the witch Pashmeira out of the kingdom and off the path of righteousness, for he believed her to be an evil witch. She lived in an abandoned church among the trees in the forest of the fallen outside the kingdom and outside the rules. Some say she put a spell on King Kurlbach, making him slave away to his lewd and lascivious behaviors, and others say lust already imprisoned the king like a ball and chain before he encountered the witch.

Upon their encounter, the king bashed and whipped Pashmeira, the witch, almost to the dying place, but stopped when his hand caught fire from her garment. She lay in agony for three days. Her tears drenched the angel's wing she rested her head on. After saying a magic prayer, a spirit helped her rise from the earth. The details of the tale vary from person to person telling the story, but one thing everyone agreed on; if the king encountered the witch Pashmeira again—one of them would surely die!

When Pashmeira traveled through the forest of the fallen, the roots underground danced beneath her feet. The earth knew her, and it knew her God. After the exile beating from the king for her evil witchcraft, the spirits led Pashmeira to the old, abandoned church hidden deep in the forest of the fallen alongside the river. No one knew exactly what happened to the churchgoers, but a graveyard rested behind the church with headstones bearing no names, only numbers. It would take great courage to enter that ghostland, as the stories told claim the graves open at night swallowing the unsuspecting and taking them down into the depths of darkness, never to return.

The gothic stone church's stain glass windows were still intact, and a weathered steeple with a giant brass bell perched high above the building. During the light of day, a kaleidoscope of colors shined vividly inside the church through the windows. Spatters of red, blue, green, yellow, and purple kissed the old wooden pews. When the wind blew strongly, the church bell rang, awakening the souls of those listening to it. Moss-covered trees and large bushes grew like shelter all around the abandoned church, keeping it hidden from plain sight.

If you looked through the beautiful windows, you'd see Pashmeira sleeping in the pastor's quarters at the back of the church. A fireplace in his former quarters kept her cauldron bubbling. If the church goers were still alive to see this, they would burn her to ashes... or take her to the king. But this old abandoned gothic church served not as her sanctuary. The forest gave her the sanctity she needed, and the river running through it gave her life. All the earth served as her altar.

Pashmeira's eyes glowed like the color of honey in the sunlight when everything felt alright, but when anything impressed not alright, they darkened black as night. She wore antlers on her head from an elk whose spirit lay dead. The sun shined through the church windows so bright; they turned the elk horns into light. On her head like stain glass, they shined with God's might, even at night. Some said her radiant, gleaming like a bearer of the light didn't cast a shadow, but a rainbow. Her skin looked like the earth and her hair like fire to your sight. Others said if you touched her enchanted garment, your hair would char, and your flesh would ignite.

Walking along the windy path in the forest of the fallen, the orange and crimson leaves crunched under the witch Pashmeira's boots. Through the trees in the distance, she saw a deer in a golden meadow at peace with the earth. A gentle breeze blew the leaves, and they skipped merrily around her in the crisp autumn air.

The sun began descending, and more leaves fluttered down from the trees like little lemon drops twirling around, glimmering with sweet light. She believed in magic, and so it was. Pashmeira reached up, capturing sunbeams in her hands. She masterfully querled the beams into threads of gold and spooled the golden thread around an old branch. She asked for more leaves to fall. They floated to the ground, lining up in the pattern of a quilt. She tailored her spun gold thread, catching every stitch by sewing the leaves together. Pashmeira joyfully carried the leaf blanket for her new guest half a league through the woods back to the abandoned church.

"He is under the king's command," Orlawn, the wise old owl, said, his many feathers blending in with the surrounding land.

The witch replied to the owl perched on her shoulder, "This I know, and you know what is written on the scroll, cannot be undone." Pashmeira's faith in her God's plan solidified in her heart like gems found under the earth.

"It is already finished," Orlawn said; his golden eyes seeing everything. He lived in the forest from the beginning. Orlawn was the forest, and the forest was Orlawn. Wisdom gifted Orlawn, and he knew every secret of the woods. It was said because of the wisdom of the owls, this was why the scribes used their quills to write with. They hoped for wisdom to depart from the feathers and permeate the parchment with truth and knowledge. The wise are gifted with truth.

Orlawn and Pashmeira journeyed further along the windy path, leaves blowing all around them. As darkness cloaked in deeper, they raptured closer to the old, abandoned church. The dry autumn wind rustled, whispering, "The time is near."

Pashmeira, the witch, gazed at the moonlight reflecting on the river water, and she said to Orlawn, "Perhaps I'll capture the moonbeams in a bucket and make a sleep potion for him."

"A sleep for the dead," Orlawn replied.

Pashmeira looked grim, like a vessel of sorrow. They passed a giant, gnarly tree with a branch that appeared like a hand. Five long finger shaped twigs scratched at the wind, and a burst of lightning struck the hand shaped branch—breaking it off from its trunk. It fell to the ground, presenting itself to Pashmeira, saying, "Please, take me!"

The Great King Kurlbach and Mobley the Friar

Much more than one thousand years ago, in a land radiating with vibrant light and undulating with deep dark magic, King Kurlbach brutally seized reign. When he did, he banished all religion being practiced. King Kurlbach's heart hardened with pride, and he decreed he would decide right from wrong. His own religion felt good in his mind and desirous in his body. "A lord is with me, and I will teach the people new ways," he said, ordering the books of the old teachings to be burned and the ashes from the burnt pages scattered over the forest of the fallen.

What the king didn't know is that words cannot truly be sundered. It can turn only the scrolls we write them on to ashes. For words do not live on parchment; they live in the hearts and minds of those who read, write, and feel them. But in the king's quest for power, he decreed that if any friar would not teach his new ways, they were to be slaughtered for their heresy. The king loved tossing bodies over the cliff into the forest of the fallen, but the witches he saved for the fire. The king hated witches, fearing they would bring about plagues in his land. 'Twas this reason he burned them, and their ashes joined the ashes of the offensive words.

When the townspeople listened closely at night, they could hear the cries from the forest of those vanished souls. The wolves picked the bodies' bones clean, and the witches and warlocks fashioned weapons from the bones and cups from their skulls. Townspeople didn't dare venture into the forest of the fallen for fear their souls too would be lost forever.

The king's most loyal friar was called Mobley, and he was quite a nervous, round little man. You'd be nervous too if you knew what the king could do. Mobley always did as the king commanded, and this autumn day the king commanded Mobley to find the witch. The king said to Mobley, "She escaped me once, but nay will it happen again."

Mobley nodded.

"When you find her, seize her and bring her before me," the king commanded.

Mobley nodded.

The king knew the power the witch possessed because he'd felt it. He contemplated sending his army out after her, but he knew a war would commence. His military still needed to recover from recent land acquisitions. The king thought if the friar could just quietly escort the witch to him, all would be his. No one needs to get hurt... yet.

The king thought he'd constructed a wise strategy to defeat the witch. He requested the friar assure the witch the King comes in love and will not harm her. Mobley would let the witch know the king's earlier grant he extended to her, still held its kindness.

The king continued, "She is evil. I should have the witch sentenced to death for her beliefs and dark magic spells, but I preach love and tolerance. For that reason and that reason only, I will pardon her from her death decree." But the king rarely spoke the truth, for he possessed a forked tongue that poked and prodded in many different directions.

The king was obsessed with the witch and thought of her day and night. The king recently dreamt of her, and in the waking hours, thoughts of her filled his head. He wanted to love her, but he did not know how... and he did not know that he did not know how.

Force did not work with the witch, and she almost set him on fire the time she stood before him in the forest. He remembered breathing in the smoke from the flames. How it burned his lungs—and stung his eyes! That could not be their last encounter. It would not be their last encounter.

Pashmeira burned the king in more ways than one. He became a king so he could conquer. He became a king so he could take whatever he wanted. He became a king so he could have much more than ordinary men. He became a king so that with the women he could buzz around like a sweet honeybee pollinating flower after flower after flower.

The king acquired many wives over the years, and when they bore him children, he gave them lilies of the valley. They draped their bodies in the finest silk. He adorned them with vines of passion flowers woven into their beautifully braided hair. The king bathed them in milk and honey before he lay with them, and he gave them gifts of silver and gold when they satisfied him. But the witch was more beautiful than the rose of Sharon, and she was the one woman to elude his touch. Dozens of flax haired women lie in wait for the king, but he longed for the fire haired witch. Behind King Kurlbach's courtyard, he kept a cache of treasure he reserved especially for Pashmeira. Once she lay with him, he would gift her rubies and diamonds.

"My lord, where am I to find this evil witch?" Mobley queried the king.

The king replied, "She lives in the shadows of the forest of the fallen, of course. Many years ago, I gave her a beating for her heresy, but a demon saved her from her fate. She did not learn her lesson, for I am told she still practices the dark magic—potions and spells from hell."

Mobley shook with terror. He would not live if he entered the forest of the fallen, he thought. The king dismissed his concerns by smattering, "The lord will be with you. Who could be against you?"

Mobley nodded.

Secretly, the king desired to steal the witch Pashmeira's garment because he heard her power lived in it. He wanted to harness her power and claim it as his own. Someone once said the Lord granted her that power. Power pleased the king. The king slaved day and night to his ego, and the power he sought held the whip. He would seize her garment from her, keep it for himself, and command her to appear before him powerless. Nothing excited the king more than this thought.

Back on the day when the king beat the witch, he watched her eyes turn black, and when he grabbed her arm, the flames of evil scorched his hand. Every time he looked at the scar on his hand, he overflowed with anger. He knew what dwelled in her. The king convinced himself it was evil that made her run from him. That evil fire starter did not belong in his kingdom. She did not belong on his earth. Without her garment, he could beat her again, and this time—to death! But not before he lay with her first, of course.

Once Mobley departed the king's majestic presence, he went to the local musty tavern to have a pint of ale, or two, or three. He believed the ale would calm his nerves, but all it did was make his belly grow. The people who frequented the tavern were a dark and rough sort of folk. All hated the king but could not speak a word against his majesty. If they did, they too would end up scattered about the forest of the fallen. Mobley knew a few of them covertly practiced the dark art of witchcraft and asked them if they knew where he could find the witch called Pashmeira. Silence tumbled over the tavern, and the air blew heavier.

A large man with rotting teeth and one eye left in his head said, "You do not want to find Pashmeira." He sipped ale from his stein.

Mobley set his fourth ale down and asked why his words would be true.

A lonely woman in the corner with a large bosom perching high above her corset told him, "She is the most powerful of them all. A twin sprouted in the womb with her, but when the midwife pulled Pashmeira's sister out, she'd been strangled with the umbilical cord. Pashmeira possesses dual powers that duel with each other. A love for the Lord and a hate for the King Kurlbach and all who do his work oozes from her."

Mobley nodded.

Two more pints of ale in his belly and Mobley stumbled from upon his tavern stool. After he hit the floor like a sack of rotten potatoes, tavern patrons laughed at him. The tavern owner rolled him out, kicking him with his booted foot. Mobley saw the ground and then the sky, the ground, and then the sky as he trundled along hearing the ridiculing roars from inside the tavern. He thought someone told a joke. The owner shouted, "No one wants you here!"

Shunned but too drunk to feel his humiliation, Mobley stood and swayed down the cobblestone road to his cottage. Spinning along, bumping into walls, he heard footsteps behind him and turned to find a young frail looking tavern wench named Emmalee following him in the darkness. She whispered, "I heard you are looking for the witch Pashmeira."

Mobley hiccupped a nod.

She instructed him, "Cross the bridge out of the kingdom and take the dark, windy path through the forest of the fallen. There you will find her at the end of it. You'll know you are getting near when you feel the chilly wind stir your soul. But be careful, for in two nights it will be All Hallows Eve, and the angered dead will walk amongst her. Take caution not to let the hand of darkness cover you with its shadow."

Mobley nodded and asked, "Should I believe everything the people tell about her spells and potions?"

The tavern wench replied, "They say she has three eyes. You cannot fool or trick her."

Mobley nodded and asked, "Do you know her?"

"When your sadness goes awry, you will know Pashmeira." After these words, Emmalee disappeared into the night.

Mobley staggered back to his cottage, and that night's ale made him feel brave enough to find the witch. He decided to save his head. Come morning, he would take the dark, windy path through the forest of the fallen and bring the witch Pashmeira to King Kurlbach.

Mobley and His Pilgrimage to Pashmeira, the Witch

The next morning, swirls of intoxication surrounded Mobley's head. Through the haze, he remembered he needed to talk the witch into appearing before the king. He clothed himself in his holy burlap gown and tied the rope under his plump waist. He hung a silver medallion of a saint around his neck and told himself he was a man of God. His nerves were frazzled, as he hadn't slept a good night's sleep since the king took reign. He poured some cream over stale bread to settle his stomach and boiled a pig's foot to sustain himself for the long walk to the witch. He dabbed holy water on his forehead, saying a prayer.

A knock at his cottage door from a mother with a baby in her arms begging for alms moved Mobley to give her half a loaf of bread and a copper coin. He dabbed holy water on her forehead, saying a prayer. He poured holy water on the baby's head, saying another prayer and sauntered down the town's cobblestone road towards the forest of the fallen.

Once at the outskirts of the forest at the edge of town, he wondered if he'd be able to find the witch. He also wondered if he'd make it out alive. He said another prayer and walked into the unknown. Surely the spirit of God would lead him safely to the witch, he thought. It didn't seem so bad. He strolled along the dirt path lined with thickets of dense trees; the squirrels gathering nuts for the winter. They scampered up and down the tree trunks with bulging cheeks. They jumped and flew from branch to branch. One pointed to the right. Mobley, looking in that direction, saw the path spun a sharp turn. This must be the dark windy path, he thought, venturing down it.

Mobley moved deeper into the forest and noticed it seemed darker. Looking up, he saw a grim sky; clouds rolling in. It would rain soon, he thought. A chill snuck up his holy gown. His legs wobbled from the cold. He continued to follow the dark dirt path as it wound around the trees. His breath labored while he waddled. He would have sworn on a stack of bibles he heard a wolf's growl. But when he looked around, he could see nothing. He felt the cold air continue to rise from the earth and creep up his tired, chubby legs. The trees lined up thicker and denser the longer he walked. When he looked up again at the sky, he could only see slivers of light, for the trees took to covering the view of the sky. He thought he heard the forest whisper to him, "Go back." Stopping to look around again, he spotted nothing. He pressed on, for if the forest of the fallen didn't kill him, surely the king would.

Mobley grew weary from the walk but knew he must continue for the king's mission. The forest grew dimmer with each step. The wind rustled the leaves, and he heard an owl hoot, crying out a hidden language to the other owls. Another owl whistled, a mournful cry of a hoot echoing in return.

A crack of thunder broke so loud it almost stopped Mobley's heart—rumbling and bursting again! When the lightning lit up the air, it made the slivers of sky between the trees turn purple. He thought he saw the shadow of a figure lurking behind a great oak tree. In a flash, it disappeared. Mobley wanted to stop and rest, but there was nowhere to lay his balding, weary head. He didn't dare stop now. It would not be safe, he thought, as he could feel his heart beating in his chest. His eyes grew accustomed to the darkness at this place in his journey. A low-hanging branch scratched his head. Confused, he thought as he wound around the dark windy path, maybe he passed the same tree more than once. The miles he traveled made him feel like he'd gone in circles. A taunting wind howled in his ears. He told himself he would not see the dead in this forest, for the Lord stayed with him. He remembered the King's words of encouragement.

Branches whipped around and the sky wailed hard. Rain drops fell all over Mobley, soaking his holy gown. Lifting his burlap robe higher than his feet, he hobbled as fast as he could down the dark, windy path. Finally, the trees broke, and he stood in a golden meadow.

Mobley saw the steeple of the abandoned church along the riverbank in the distance, poking up high above the wall of trees surrounding it. The fierce autumn wind blew the church bell back and forth... back and forth. When he listened to the resounding gongs at twilight, Mobley heard the call of the Lord. His soul stirred as heaven's bells serenaded him. The beauty of the forest looked like heaven on earth. The sound of unbroken joy from his deliverer rang out! He hurried towards the church, thinking this must be where the witch lives.

In the years following this day, townspeople told a tale of hell's bells ringing for Mobley. For autumn is the season of deception. We are so enamored of her beauty; her fallen leaves seem not like death at all. The grave waited patiently to collect Mobley in its decrepit arms.

Mobley the Friar and Pashmeira the Witch Meet

Mobley jaunted toward the church, and rain pelted his balding, weary head. An owl gliding quickly past his face startled him. The owl flew higher, circling around the church. Mobley trenched along through the bushes getting scratched and tumbling along the way. Finally, he arrived at the large Gothic door to the church. Finding it opened a crack, Mobley wondered if the door led into darkness. He stopped dead in his tracks; his sandals drenched. He stood at the door waiting and wondering if he should knock, but the sound of the rain pounded so loudly he couldn't hear himself think clearly. If he turned back now, the king would chop his head off. Mobley quite liked his balding, weary head.

Pashmeira stood under a tree behind Mobley, wondering how long Mobley would stand at the open door before going in. Pleased to have this visitation, she asked, "Dear sir, may I help you?"

Her voice frightened Mobley, and for protection, his trembling hands clutched the silver medallion hanging around his neck.

Slowly, he turned around and saw her. She wasn't a myth. He saw her for real flesh and blood standing there in front of him. He quickly recalled all the dark tales told of her. She did not look at all like he thought she would. She didn't have three eyes. Beautiful of face, she seemed so understanding, and her long hair gave an image of warm flames dancing around her shoulders, smoldering down her back. Gazing at the stain glass antlers on her head enamored Mobley. Light glowing all around them cast a mosaic essence everywhere. Her bountifully filled out garment drew him in. There were no dark shadows around her. Speechless, he stepped towards her.

As she waited for Mobley to speak, Orlawn landed on Pashmeira's shoulder. If Mobley had a hand to harm her, Orlawn's fixed stare wouldn't miss even the first second of it. Drizzling rain spoke knowledge to Orlawn, and the wind whispered wisdom in his ears.

Mobley queried, "Are you the witch they call Pashmeira?"

To which the witch replied, "I am."

Mobley said, "I have come to bring you to the king. He has summoned you to his presence." Mobley thought he heard a wolf's growl again, but when he turned and peered into the woods, he could see nothing.

"This will not happen, for there is another plan 'twas already finished," Pashmeira said, tilting her head with a hint of a smile resting at her lips. She looked away and saw a goat standing under a tree in the distance, half his face covered in shadow and his Billy-beard five inches in length. With horns pointing back, the goat chewed the grass around his hooved feet.

"You look like a fine lady and not a witch, but if I have to take you back by force, I will," Mobley informed her.

"As I said, this will not happen. Let's go inside to take shelter from the rain. Come, warm yourself by the fire. I will brew you a cup of tea." The witch walked past Mobley into the old stone church with a rickety leaking wooden roof towering above her.

Mobley nodded and eagerly followed her in.

Her gentle footsteps echoed through the holy house. A scared little gray mouse scurried out from under a pew, taking refuge in a hole in the church's stone wall.

Mobley didn't want to take the witch forcibly. He wanted her to go willingly and face her sins. Perhaps he could convince her of this over a cup of tea. Mobley could see rows and rows of old empty wooden pews dimly lit by candles in the church. With rain pelting the church's stain glass windows from dark gray storm clouds, they could not be seen through. The altar stood tall at the front of the church. The place for sacrifices awaited its spoils.

They processioned down the middle aisle to arrive at the back quarters. A fire flickered under a bubbling cauldron. She placed a sash of tea leaves in a skull cup; open sockets plugged by rocks. Pashmeira, the witch, ladled some boiling water into the cranium cup. She gave the warm tea to Mobley who appeared to be afraid to take it. "I assure you it is harmless," she said, her voice full of mercy. "We don't much think about our bones, do we? Not unless the ache or break."

She seemed to not be wet at all, Mobley thought, while he felt his drenched burlap robe scratch and cling to his pudgy skin. He shivered from the cold, saying, "Thank you. People don't care for me much."

Orlawn perched on a window ledge, silent and watching Mobley.

Mobley took the skull and sat on a rocking chair. The witch stood before him as he drank. The tea soothed Mobley.

"You must have gotten terribly cold out on the dark, windy path. It can be a bit chilly out there this time of year, and the wind is downright wicked," she said to him.

Mobley nodded.

"You must be tired from such a long walk."

Mobley nodded.

"If you would like to rest before your journey back, you may," Pashmeira said, pointing toward a feather pillow bed in the corner.

"I think I might," Mobley mumbled as his eyelids quickly grew heavy. He laid down on the soft feather bed. Pashmeira reached for a flute to make music, and the sound from it soothed Mobley's soul so that he fell into a deep sleep. The witch covered him with the blanket of leaves she had sewed the day before. The sacred earth gave them up for his warmth and rest.

Mobley's Dream

After several hours of sleep, Pashmeira pulled back the leaf blanket and removed Mobley's wet clothing. When she did this, Mobley awoke. As he lay there naked, he watched her hang his robe over the rocking chair in front of the fire to dry. His arousal growing, he watched her remove her own garment, exposing her body to him. She removed her antlers that were woven into a leather strap tied around her head. Next to him, she felt warm. Mobley could not resist, and he took the witch Pashmeira. When he was done, he fell asleep once more. The witch got up, put her garment and antlers back on, and covered Mobley with the gold threaded leaf blanket. His passionate release led him into a deep sleep.

When he awoke the next morning, he remembered his dream. He felt disappointed the intimacy had not been real, or so he thought. Orlawn perched at the window. Pashmeira rocked in the rocking chair in front of the fire, drinking tea. The rain ceased. Mobley's holy robe was dry and on his body. Feeling embarrassed and ashamed of his dream, he sat up and pushed the blanket aside.

"Are you feeling better?" Pashmeira, the witch, asked. "You slept for quite a while."

Mobley nodded. Now it was time to tell the witch she would need to come with him, but before he could say it, she spoke, "I will not be leaving with you. If you try to take me with you, Orlawn's talons will gouge out your eyes. Is your king worth your sight?"

Mobley shook his head. He tried to think clearly but felt confused once more. He thought perhaps he could tell the king he could not find the witch.

"You are welcome to stay a while longer. We'll be having rabbit stew tonight in celebration of All Hallows Eve," she said.

"That sounds delicious." He couldn't wait to feast with the witch, for no one ever invited him to feast.

Pashmeira handed Mobley a cup filled with goat's milk mixed with honey. "I am sure you are hungry."

Grateful, Mobley took the cup and gulped it.

Pashmeira went out into the forest to catch a rabbit. Orlawn flew behind her. The friar stayed inside the church, still thinking about his dream. She felt so real; he thought. He wandered into the sanctuary and stared up at the stain glass windows. In the light of day, he could see everything. All the saints depicted in the windows made him feel he was not alone. Walking to the altar, he saw there was one candle lit. The flame flickered and danced. He wondered whose soul the candle had been lit for, not knowing it was his. Looking back up at the stain glass windows, he stood in the light and with a heavy heart he took in every detail; his favorite depiction being of a dove ascending into the sky. He thought of his faith and how quickly he abandoned it upon the threat of death. The other friars fought so much harder than he. Perhaps he should not have told the king of this church he heard about in the forest worshiping a God the king denounced, but it put Mobley in such good standing with the king. Mobley often tried to hide his dark deed from the Lord, but as we all know, nothing is ever hidden from the Lord.

Walking along the damp earth, Orlawn asked Pashmeira, "Why did you invite him to dinner?"

"He needs a friend before he dies," the witch replied.

"This land has nothing but small kings." Orlawn fluttered his feathers, covering Pashmeira in the shadow of his wings.

They traveled past the meadow and along the river. Rays of autumn sunlight hit the water, making it look like liquid gold. They traveled further down another path to a ditch with a well perched at the cleft. The rabbits jumped about on each other and never saw Orlawn glide in. Orlawn captured two rabbits, one in each of his claws.

Pashmeira began preparing the stew. In a beautiful basket she wove in the springtime, she gathered the last of her onions, carrots, parsnips, sage, and pumpkins she'd grown in her garden from seeds she planted two seasons earlier. At the edge of her garden, she placed seven hazelnuts on a shard of broken mirror for her little feathered friend who would visit soon. She closed her eyes and heard the caw, caw, caw in the distance, signaling he was on his way.

Crueneilious the crow possessed the habit of lurking around the outside of the king's castle. Fancy shiny items caught the attention of his black, glassy, marble-like eyes. With his clever claws, he swiftly snatched up treasures. That autumn day, he perched quietly on the windowsill of the king's royal seamstress, waiting for her to depart her chamber. Once she did, he poked his long beak through the iron protection bars over her window. Beak clinking against the bars, he plucked up her brass thimble.

In flight to Pashmeira, he carried the royal thimble back to the old, abandoned church, clinching it tightly in his pointy beak. Landing at the edge of the garden, Crueneilious dropped the thimble down by the shard of mirror and ate his hazelnuts.

"Thank you, my love," Pashmeira said, picking up the thimble and examining her new ornate gift.

With the thimble in her pocket, she roamed the land and found two dried, knotted sticks. While rubbing them together to start a fire, Pashmeira recited her witch's chant:

"Friction, friction, smoke, and fire,
Feel the heat burning your feet.
Raising up from the ground
raging flames consuming the earth abound
bringing you down, down
into the depths of hell.
For this reason, we cast a spell
to ignite the power
at the witching hour.
In us is a sword bearing spirit.
It's calling.
Do you hear it?"

Flames swirled around the dried sticks, and Pashmeira placed them on top of some brush covered logs. Boiling the rabbit meat with the vegetables and sage in a second cauldron she kept outside filled the air with the scent of Mobley's last supper. She prepared a pumpkin bread with grains from her harvest and an egg from a wild chicken she captured and housed in the church. She added a drizzle of maple syrup she tapped from a tree. Holding an old, jagged knife, she carved a face into the hollow pumpkin, making quite a scary-looking jack-o'-lantern. A lit candle in the center of it made its eyes and mouth flicker.

Sometime later, the wolf Warlawrn smelled the stew and so did Bertchwald, the bear. They roamed towards the outdoor fire.

In the evening, after the stew had been cooked for a few hours, Pashmeira let Mobley know it was time for the meal. They sat outside by a bonfire. Warlawrn, the wolf approached them; his sky-blue eyes glowing in the dark. Mobley shouted a cry of fear.

Pashmeira said, "It is alright. He is my friend."

"You are friends with a wolf?"

The witch replied, "You wouldn't want him to be an enemy."

Warlawrn growled a warning at Mobley, a slow, deep growl that exposed his sharp fangs. The bushes rustled, and Bertchwald the bear appeared grunting as he moved his big furry body along. Mobley froze, turning white.

"Do not fear. He is also my friend," the witch said.

Breathless, Mobley asked, "You are friends with a bear?"

"You wouldn't want to be enemies with him, either." The witch smiled.

The Bonfire

The witch ladled rabbit stew into a skull cup and served her guest Mobley. Mobley thought it to be the best stew he ever tasted. The witch ladled a bowl of stew for each the owl, the wolf, and the bear. She scratched behind Warlawrn the wolf's ear and under his chin before she served him; this the wolf loved her for.

Bertchwald the bear slurped his stew but thought only of honey. Oh, how he wished he could delight in some honey for dessert. Perhaps the witch would serve some? The desire for honey tethered Bertchwald to the witch. Not her love, but the honey.

Orlawn the owl watched Pashmeira as she sat in front of the fire. Orlawn loved to look upon her and watch over her. He asked for nothing in return from her... other than for her to obey his words of warning and wisdom.

As Mobley chewed rabbit between his yellow teeth, he too stared at the witch from across the other side of the fire. He thought he saw the shadow of a demon appear and stand behind her. He blinked. It disappeared.

Pashmeira, the witch, asked Mobley, "The demons have presented themselves to you, haven't they?"

Mobley nodded.

Pashmeira said, "Everyone has spirits around them. Some of us can see them, and some of us can't." She served him a piece of pumpkin cake. Mobley gobbled it up and rested his hand on a rock next to him. He thought he heard a scream and quickly pulled his hand away. Pashmeira asked, "You can hear the rocks, can't you?"

Mobley nodded.

Pashmeira explained, "As rocks are formed from changes in the earth over time, they observe the sins committed on the soil. If you listen closely, you can hear what they've seen. They'll tell you the secrets of the land."

"I feel so far from God out here in this dark forest," Mobley said.

"You are closer to Him than you think," Pashmeira replied.

Mobley picked up the rock and held it to his ear. He gasped and threw it down.

Pashmeira knew the rocks spoke boldly on All Hallows Eve. She inquired, "Please tell me, sir, who does your king say I am?"

Mobley answered, "He says you are a heretic and practice evil. He says you are a witch."

Upon hearing this, the bear reared up and stood eleven feet tall on his hind legs, growling so loud it almost cracked Mobley's ear drum. Mobley trembled with terror. The witch shook her head at the bear, and Bertchwald backed down.

She asked Mobley, "And who do you say I am?"

Mobley looked at her beautifully warm face lit up by the light of the fire flames and her eyes glowed like sweet honey. He replied, "You appear to me as a lady of the night." Mobley felt confused again. His dream was so real in his mind he thought it to be true, and she must be a prostitute. She would need to be paid for what she did for him the night before, but he gave his last copper coin to a beggar. When Mobley looked at Warlawrn, he saw the wolf laugh. Mobley blinked, and the wolf moved closer to Pashmeira. She rested her hand on the wolf's back, petting him.

The flames of the fire danced around, flickering back and forth. The skulls on the ground glowed with the firelight. Mobley felt a chill from within and all around. Orlawn kept his eyes on Mobley. He could eat later.

The witch asked Mobley, "Do you know when death waits for someone?"

Mobley shook his head.

"I do," Pashmeira said. "And death waits closely next to you."

Mobley reminded her, "You said if I did not force you out of the forest of the fallen, that you would spare my life."

The witch smiled. "I will honor that, but it is not I who will take your life."

Mobley looked at the owl, and then the wolf, and lastly, the bear.

The witch said, "It is not them either."

She stood. Her cauldron now empty, she walked to the life-giving river and filled a skull cup with water. She poured it into her pot. Holding a branch from a willow tree, she drew a square in the surrounding dirt hanging cauldron. Into the water she sprinkled wild rose petals, sprigs of jasmine, cinnamon sticks, sagebrush, and a bit of magic. While it bubbled, she chanted:

**"The men will fall soon
under the red moon.
God of earth
give us a new birth."**

She ladled tea for Mobley and herself. Mobley drank it all in, thinking how sweet her feet were to carry this lovely cup of tea to him.

Bertchwald, the bear, moved towards an old giant kettledrum sitting on the ground near the fire, and with his black clawed paws, he began pounding on it with a rhythm and force that made the ground shake. The unearthed dirt sifted about, and trees swayed in the wind. Smoke from the gleaming fire transcended into the sky, signaling heaven needed a sacrifice.

Inoculated by terror, Mobley trembled at what his eyes revealed to him. How could a bear pound a drum?

The witch said, "The drumbeat keeps away unwanted forces. It's a warning call on All Hallows Eve."

"Your All Hallows Eve is a pagan holiday. It is not holy! What do you know of holiness?" Mobley asked.

"We honor the dead around here," Pashmeira said. "Those who walked the earth before us have something to tell us, and death teaches us how to live."

Mobley protested, "The saints do not know you. Only the demons know you."

"The Lord lets the dark and the light walk this earth together. If that pleases the Lord to allow this, who are you to judge it?" Pashmeira asked.

"But why would you call darkness upon you?"

Pashmeira answered, "You don't want to invite darkness in, but if by ignorance you do, there is one and only one weapon to fight it with."

"Light triumphs over darkness. This is in the King's good book, and you should not be reading stars to tell you the future," Mobley replied.

"If we could travel through the sky to the stars, it would take us to the future. They are already there waiting for us. God's love for us is written in the stars. I believe in a God that knows the mystery of time. God is in every piece of this earth. Who is man to make up God's rules? The earth sings of the glory of God. The heavenly stars are above the earth and know everything under it. Men scribed these tales, and your king burned their words and made up his own. He said ancient stories couldn't teach us anything. Tell me, dear Mobley, what makes a person holy?"

Mobley answered, "When there is no sin in him."

"You think you have not one bad thing in you?"

Mobley stated proudly, "God granted me knowledge. This is what I have."

"Do you have Spirit?" Pashmeira asked.

"I have good spirit in me, but you would not know this, for the king says you have bad spirit in you."

"Knowledge is only in the mind, but wisdom is in the heart. Spirit is when heart and mind unite. This is what I know of Spirit," Pashmeira said. She stood, and her bountiful garment unwound from her body, leaving her as naked as the day her mother bore her.

Orlawn kept watch on Mobley.

Warlawrn the wolf looked at Mobley, licking his chops. Warlawrn pretended not to see the witch's unclothed body.

Bertchwald pounded the drum harder, making the earth rumble.

Pashmeira moved her alluring body to the rhythm of the drum, dancing around the fire, and Mobley looked upon her. Her bare hips swirled around in the night sky. The witch asked Mobley, "Do you know why flames flicker?"

Mobley shook his head.

"As the light of truth tries to escape the flames, the darkness pulls it back in and tries to put it out... just like the constant spiritual battle raging all around us."

Pashmeira's antlers glimmered rays of white speckled light into the night. The frosty moon shined on her, and the stars came down from the sky, moving around her. Mobley stood, took off his holy robe, and danced with the witch. This time, he knew the wolf laughed at him. His naked body flapped around, and the drumbeat seemed to control his movements. He gyrated behind the witch with much pleasure. He knew she had caught him under some sort of spell, otherwise he wouldn't be doing this. After the dancing came the singing. Mobley echoed the lyrics the rocks sang out:

"Our joy is to be of the earth,
strewn about the ground.
But man came down,
turned us around,
and tore apart our land
by his selfish hand.
Now we have no home.
For these sins, we will atone."

They sang and danced under the moonlight for quite a while. The light of the fire cast shadows all around them. The songs of passion Mobley felt deep in his throbbing loins. As Mobley succumbed to his lust for Pashmeira, the stones around them blushed, looking not their way. The autumn wind exhaled, and leaves blew onto the surface of the river. Golden leaves gently floated on the water under the moonlight. Crickets chirped their harmony, and the willow trees by the riverbank whistled in the breeze.

The Exodus Out of the Forest of the Fallen

When Mobley awoke the next morning in his holy robe, he remembered the singing and the dancing... and the gyrating. He laid on the ground in front of the fire that dwindled down. The smoke still smoldered from the ashy earth below. The scent filled his nostrils, and Pashmeira presented herself to him like a burnt offering. She wore her fitted garment and gave him another cup of tea. "It is time for you to leave the forest of the fallen," she said.

The bear was gone.

The wolf was gone.

The owl sat perched on a rock that could tell a noble tale.

Orlawn could tell his own not so noble tale of what really happened in the night. While everyone slept, he silently flew to the king's castle. He saw the goings on there. The king lay with one of his most beautiful flax haired wives.

King Kurlbach whispered to her, "I love you the most, my dove."

His wife knew the delicacy of the king's ego. For encouragement in the throes of their passion, she cried out to the king, "Your majesty! No one does this better than you!"

Upon completion, the angered king asked her, "How would you know this?"

His beautiful wife gasped at his question. The king cast her into prison to be shut up for the rest of her days, and he ordered his army to get him five new flax haired concubines from the neighboring town. The king lovingly tended to all of them, telling them he would love them all equally.

Orlawn now stared at Mobley in the morning light, dark shadows casting from him.

Mobley lifted his aging plump body off the ground and drank the tea. It revived him.

Pashmeira said, "Orlawn and I will walk with you back down the dark, windy path to the bridge leading to the kingdom. If you go by yourself, you will not make it out alive. The unwanted forces know you are here, and they have no rest on All Saints' Day."

Mobley fearfully nodded.

They began their journey out of the forest of the fallen, along the trail lined by stones leading out from the church to the forest. They cried a warning to Mobley. The ears upon Mobley's balding weary head could not auscultate the cautionary tale.

Every tree seemed to look the same to Mobley. The sunshine-colored leaves fluttered from all the trees. Orlawn flew in circles overhead in the cold dry air around them, keeping a close watch. Pashmeira stayed by Mobley's side. They made their way quietly along the path as it wound around and around the thickets of trees endlessly.

The air from the ground grew colder when they got deeper into the dark, windy path. That chilly autumn day, a soft warm orange glow of light gleamed all around them from Pashmeira's antlers. It was as if one saint from the image on the stain glass church window showed them the way through the forest. Could this be the path of life? Was John the Baptist pointing the way? Mobley wondered. He feared to wonder too long because the king banished that old offensive religion.

A hoot from Orlawn signaled Pashmeira to thrust down the hand branch broom she'd picked up the day before. When the hand branch broom hit the ground, it grabbed a snake by the head and choked it with its twiggy fingered grip, sweeping the serpent's destruction away from them. Once the snake lived not, the broom sprang back into Pashmeira's hand.

Mobley looked at Pashmeira in shock and disbelief from what he saw. "Magic?"

Pashmeira felt sad for Mobley did not know the power.

Mobley preached to Pashmeira the witch, "The dark evil black arts are from the devil! You will receive eternal damnation!"

Pashmeira replied, "I have no power the Lord does not give me. Perhaps it was the hand of God that saved you from the serpent?"

Mobley queried, "A power from the Lord? I do not have this power."

Pashmeira smiled. "You have not, because you ask not."

Mobley declared, "The magic power you have is evil! My beautiful lady, you know not what you do. You should repent! I knew of your mother, and she, too, was a witch. I did not know of your father."

"You do know my Father, and sometimes good uses evil to defeat evil."

"This is not truth!"

"The truth rings out louder than the church bells. When I was lost, heaven called me out of darkness into the light. Dear Mobley, when the enemy comes knocking, will you be prepared?"

When Mobley walked the wrong way through a dangerous marsh, the hand branch broom clutched his arm, leading him the right way. After several miles of walking, Mobley asked the witch, "Are you sure you won't come with me to see the king? He will gift you with an abundance of riches. There is only one path to righteousness, and it is the King's way. His teachings are pure and true. He preaches love and tolerance."

"Can your king's god bring the bones in the forest of the fallen back to life?"

"Who can raise the dead?" Mobley wondered.

Pashmeira asked, "Tell me, how many wives does the king have now?"

Mobley stopped walking and looked at the witch. "One hundred and seventy-five," he replied, "but these women would have no home if the king had not taken care of them. The king has been nothing but gracious and logical about it. He says he loves all his wives equally."

Pashmeira looked at Mobley closely, her honey-colored eyes turned black. "If logic is your king, intuition is my queen. Spirit tells me I have all the abundance I need. Your king has made a parfait of lies with layers of deception, causing terror among the people. Truth is a gift your king does not have."

Mobley trembled. "The king will have your head, dear lady, if you keep talking like that!"

"And how many heretics has your king murdered?"

"Murder is such a gruesome word. He has executed those deserving of it, and I have not been able to keep count, but I am sure they deserved their punishment," Mobley answered, wringing his hands; his fingers turning like a weathervane in a fierce, wicked storm.

"The king devours our liberty, but I will find a way to get it back. I will use his lasciviousness as a weapon against him. If a king cannot control his loins, he cannot truly be king." Pashmeira reached into the pocket of her garment and clutched the ornate compass inside. "Your king brought chaos, death, and lies. My King brings order, life, and truth. I bear the light and will restore this!"

"The king believes his god is the only god, and your God is a false god," Mobley warned.

"Your king taxes the poor further into poverty, making them pay for his filthy life. My King preaches a truth for all, yet we all stand collected on this same earth while your king lives like a pig, believing he can sit in judgement of the rest of us. Mere men merely seek to live a good life, but small kings seek to destroy. Keep your eyes on the King for your king's days will see an end."

"My lady, the king has a power you cannot fight. I fear you will lose your life if you try," Mobley warned, feeling afraid for the witch.

"To die is to gain, and the hand of God will fight my battles. I have nothing to fear."

The friar replied, "You have a tongue of fire that will consume you, my lady. Quiet your mouth before it leads you to the gallows. The king persecutes all who talk like you."

"You cannot silence my words of truth. Once they're spoken, you will hear them from everlasting to everlasting," Pashmeira said.

"The shadow of death is cast over you. I've seen it."

"Dear Mobley, I am a daughter of the light."

They traveled again, silenced by Spirit, until they finally got to the edge of the forest of the fallen. The squirrels scampered up and down the trees franticly, their cheeks ready to burst from their successful nutty harvest. They dashed and stashed all around. The neighboring town could be seen in the distance, and Mobley felt remorseful he could not take the witch with him. Pashmeira spoke farewell to Mobley. "Remember, dear Mobley, heaven knows your name, and death is not the end." An east wind blew, and she blended back into the forest of the fallen.

Mobley slowly walked along the bridge by himself... it creaked with every step he took. A troll with an orange face and emerald-green eyes grabbed Mobley's foot. Startled, Mobley drew back.

"Be careful, for you are in great danger!" the troll warned.

Mobley hurried over the bridge, seeing the light from the kingdom for a moment when he got back on the cobblestone road. In a flash—Orlawn swooped down and gouged out both of Mobley's eyes! In pain and darkness, Mobley wailed and flailed about, blinking, and feeling the stabbing pain. Blood flowed from his barren sockets and ran down his ruddy cheeks. Townspeople rushed to Mobley's aid when they heard his agonizing screams.

Pashmeira, deep in the forest on the other side of the bridge when this happened, stopped in her tracks and waited for Orlawn. Orlawn glided a landing on her right shoulder with bloody talons gently gripping. She asked him why he took the friar's eyes.

Orlawn replied, "I am a jealous owl, and no other wisdom besides mine will be preached to you. He will not evangelize his king's false religion to you again. You granted Mobley hospitality, and how did he repay you? His eyes made him see filthy things, so I plucked them out. He will never see you unclothed again."

"His mind saw me unclothed, not his eyes."

Orlawn turned his head to the side and replied, "That man had holy water dripping from his forehead but hell fire blazing in his heart. Your neck is in danger, and he knows this. His lips ooze with lies, and his hands tried to carry out evil deeds for the king. He sold the sacrifice of his own people for a place of prestige in an evil kingdom. He tried to harm my disciple. I, in turn, harmed him."

Mobley's Fate

The townspeople aided Mobley in his agony. They cleaned his eye sockets and wrapped a cloth around his head to keep his eyes covered. They led him to the king as he requested. Once standing before the king in his courtyard, Mobley spoke, "My lord and my king, I could not bring the evil witch back to you. Her owl, he's evil too, and as you can see, he plucked my eyes out when I tried."

"Yes, unlike you, I can see," the king said, feeling no sympathy for Mobley in his failure to complete the mission. A failure could not be tolerated. In the king's mind, this made Mobley as evil as the witch. What an embarrassment to his kingdom that an owl got the best of this friar. The king spoke again, "Tell me, before you lost your sight, what did the witch look like?"

Mobley answered, "Oh, she has hair like fire and wears antlers that look like pieces of stained glass. They shine all around her. She's glorious!"

The king asked, "And her garment, what did that look like?"

Mobley answered, "'Twas the colors of the autumn leaves and lined with gold. It was like the warm blanket she covered me with on her enchanting soft bed."

This angered the king, and he burned with jealousy. He thought of the crown on his head and couldn't believe Mobley would have the gall to do what he did. The king asked, "You lay in her bed?"

Mobley thought to lie about where he lay but could not. He confessed, "I did! I partook in her flesh twice, but not thrice!"

The king, burning with anger, inquired, "Where was this witch's bed you laid in?"

"In that old, abandoned church in the forest of the fallen. The church you slew," Mobley answered.

King Kurlbach queried, "The church that would not abandon their beliefs for my commanded teachings? The one you told me about?"

"I betrayed the church for you my lord," Mobley said, ringing his hands like dirty laundry he could not get clean while he stood in total blind darkness.

"And now you have betrayed me too," the king said, nodding to one of his guards. The guard handed the king a noose.

Mobley objected, "You are still my king, your majesty. I assure you I have not betrayed you."

The king approached Mobley. "Since you lay with her, you are as evil as her. If I were to spare your life, you would spread a plague across my kingdom just like she would, and I cannot have that." With ruthless hands, the king put the noose in Mobley's trembling hands and said, "You know what to do with this."

The rope, like a snake coiling around Mobley's hands, waited to inflict a venomous bite. Mobley could see no way out for himself. He slipped the noose around his neck, wondering if the Lord would ever forgive him for what he did.

The guard tended to Mobley, making sure the rope seized the breath in his body until his protesting mouth went silent and cold.

After Mobley's flesh wilted to the gallows, the king burned Mobley's lifeless body. If he lay with a witch, he was a witch. While stoking the fire, the king looked into the flames and thought he saw the witch's black eyes staring back at him. The king jumped, and the eyes vanished. For a moment, he wondered what the truth in all of this was. The king's fear hid behind his anger. Scattering Mobley's ashes in a rage, the king spit out, "Good riddance."

The fierce, flourishing wind carried the ashes to the ghostland graveyard. Burned bone particles drifted to the ground and darkness shut in. The headstones rose taller. A purple fog rolled around the graveyard. The numbers turned to names, and the names on the headstones cried out. They shrieked like the night the king's army slaughtered them.

Pashmeira stood at her bubbling cauldron, and a vision of Mobley's body burning flashed before her. She closed her eyes and heard the cries from the cemetery. Grief shook her, and sadness smoldered around her. Mobley's soul agglutinated to the forest of the fallen, and an autumn death descended over everything. The unwanted forces were victorious that day... or were they?

The Wolf's Winter Solstice

THE WOLF

Warlawrn was the wolf, and oh what warrior of a wolf he was!

The spirit of a warrior he possessed,

and a fire for hunting burned in his chest.

The winter belonged to Warlawrn,

for hibernation was not a luxury to keep him warm.

Winter left him cold, bitter,

and a lot thinner.

A few times, the winter almost took him under

with force, like thunder.

He was the leader of his pack,

always leading the attack.

When he looked at you,

his hunger grew.

Saliva dripped from his jaws,

and out of his paws poked his sharp claws.

He first calculated the take down in his mind.

You would be devoured. It was just a matter of time.

He loved the thrill

of the kill.

He traipsed through the snowy mud

in search of prey until his fangs were covered with blood.

His fur was as black as night,

he gave the other animals quite a fright

right before he took a bite

with all his might.

He'd rip their flesh from side to side,

tearing off their hide.

Warlawrn was strong, quick, and brave.

When he was done with you,

there were no bones left for the grave.

More than the other wolves, he was older,

but if you challenged him, he could roll you off a cliff, making you drop

like a boulder.

Warlawrn never led his pack astray,

and the she-wolves always stayed.

Warlawrn howled at the moon,

making the she-wolves swoon.

He drove them crazy,

for Warlawrn was a handsome wolf, and at the mating he was never lazy.

Meet him out between the trees,

if you please.

When Warlawrn met the witch

down in a snow-covered ditch,

she looked at his fangs that could pierce like a knife

and quickly end her life.

She looked into his black eyes.

They turned as blue as the skies.

One eye turned first,

like a shooting starburst.

With two different colored eyes, he could see heaven and hell

From the cast of a witch's spell.

If one eye stayed blue and the other turned back to black,

you better watch your back!

Heaven cast a rainbow across his fur,

and the witch said, "For my heartache, you are to be the cure."

Warlawrn knew

what she said rang true.

The wolf answered, "If you will help me through the winter, your

friendship I will take,

and I will help you with your heartache."

The King's Assignment to Underlin the Soldier

The king's anger blazed in his heart, and the smoke from that fire clouded his brain with fury. While waiting for his cupbearer, he thought if Mobley couldn't do the assignment, he'd find a stronger friar to take down the witch. Yes, that would be his next move.

The king's cupbearer, a trustworthy man indeed, held a soft cloth in his noble hand, gently wiping the outside of King Kurlbach's goblet. He meticulously cleaned the royal cup dusted in gold, etched with leaves and vines, and studded with precious jewels. Turning the cloth over, he rubbed the inside until it shined with glory. Filling a decanter full of the wine, he let it breathe. After waiting the proper amount of time, the cupbearer poured himself a sip of the finest wine in the land. It pleased him to sniff the vintage. Holding his sip of wine in a lesser cup than the king's, he swirled it around, and swallowed.

He waited.

And waited.

No poison.

He filled the king's gold goblet with the wine and, taking great care, he carried it to the king's throne, setting it at the king's right hand. "I think you will like the wine from this batch, your majesty." The cupbearer stepped back.

King Kurlbach lifted the heavy cup to his corrupted lips and drank. "This is a fine fermentation. You are dismissed."

Several weeks after Mobley's execution, the king employed a new friar. He came from a foreign land, and he was called Underlin. A soldier he was, posing as a friar, for he desperately wanted the mission. Courageous and noble, he desired nothing more than to aid the king. He carried a sharp sword and huge calves strode up his legs. Fearing not an owl as Mobley did, he would bring the witch back to the king and end her evil ways. Underlin knew he'd be rewarded with a high honor if he did this deed, for the king told him so. The head of the king's army possessed riches far greater than anyone else in the army and owned several wives, for the king paid him well.

Underlin inquired of the king, "Would you spare one of your wives for me as I am a lonely, noble man? I would even take a concubine as a wife."

The king smirked and said, "I cannot spare a wife or a concubine for you, but I can give you a chest of silver and gold if you bring the witch before me. This should not be a problem for someone as strong as you. Mobley failed because he was weak." In his heart, the king knew this was not true. The king knew the power the witch possessed, for he had felt it for a few brief fleeting moments.

Underlin asked, "Is it true the witch can spin the sunbeams into gold?"

The king replied, "'Tis not her gold I am after." He sipped from his royal goblet, enjoying a finer batch than the last.

Underlin accepted the king's mission and believed he would complete it with ease. He too was told by the townspeople to travel to the edge of town, cross the bridge and take the dark, windy path through the forest to the place where you feel your soul stir. The strategy he planned required him to bring a bow and arrows to kill the owl.

The autumn days briskly surrendered to winter, and Underlin needed to journey into the forest of the fallen before the snow season came.

Because winter would take over soon, Bertchwald, his lady bear, and cubs went into hibernation. They ate a feast of salmon, grass, berries, and roots before laying down on the earth of his cave at the top of a vast mountain. Secluded from the rest of the forest, it would protect them from the winter elements during their peaceful slumber.

Orlawn retreated to his great oak tree to help his parliament and tend to his female owl. His parliament needed his guidance, and his female owl needed his love. The wisdom of the owls was born out of lives fully lived and taking in the lessons from the surrounding forest.

When not staying warm in his own winter cave, Warlawrn led the hunt for his pack. Three new pups romped around him and his she-wolf. They brought down a stag with antlers that curved in towards each other in the shape of a heart. This was all that was left after the wolves devoured him. They ground his bones between their teeth. Their meals were getting fewer and farther in between. Nothing was to be wasted.

Pashmeira gathered as much wood as she could to store in the old, abandoned stone church. Plucking up the last of the honeycombs, she found and tapped another maple tree. Drying some meat, salmon, tea leaves, berries, and herbs, she also stored up grains, nuts, and seeds in buckets and sewed more blankets. She made candles from bees' wax and said another magic prayer for the winter solstice.

With Pashmeira's triune tribe of forest animals retreating to their winter homes, that left her alone with the church mouse. During most of the long, cold winter nights, the mouse she named Monstros would be her only companion. He squeaked through the sanctuary, letting her know when he was around. Monstros was a bit afraid of her and ran around quickly underfoot. He didn't eat much, just a few crumbs were all he asked for.

Pashmeira fashioned herself a new winter cloak using thick midnight blue fabric she found in the back of the church. Perhaps the fabric had been used as a shroud. Wearing the royal thimble, she tediously fastened white feathers one by one to the collar. While she sewed, she chanted:

"Thimble, thimble,
worn like a symbol.
The feathers of a dove I sew
onto the cloak they appear white as snow.
With spirit and fire
end a sinful desire."

Winter would be hard on all of them, except Bertchwald; he slept peacefully while the rest of them fought to survive the cold. For winter is the season that demands to be taken seriously. If not, she will freeze you out with her chilling silence.

Underlin Makes His Way to the Witch

Underlin, the mighty soldier, navigated through the dark, windy forest with ease. It seemed nonsense to him that an owl could stop a man. He made his way through the forest of the fallen, and the unwanted forces were aware of his presence. They let him pass. He felt the cold come up from the ground, but this only made him move faster. When a snake slithered in front of him, he took out his sword and swiftly cut off its head. Triumphantly, he marched on. He marched through the thickets of trees and marshes of mud. He wound around and around and down to the riverbank. As he approached it, he looked up and saw the abandoned church steeple standing high above the walls of trees surrounding it. The wind blew the bell, and he felt his soul stir.

He smiled, knowing the mission was close to being completed.

While Underlin forged through the forest, Pashmeira crafted a winter wreath by winding around twigs and tiny branches to form a small circle no bigger than a crown. She plucked evergreen branches and wove them into the wreath. She picked crimson-colored berries from a holly plant, sticking them into the circle of sticks. The pine scent permeated the air. She pricked her finger on one of the pointy holly leaves and a few drops of her blood dripped onto the wreath. She hung the wreath on the front of the old wooden church door, leaving the door ajar for her visitor.

Underlin moved quickly through the trees, overgrown bushes, and ferns in front of the church. When he got to the huge wooden inset door to the front of the dark stone church, he stood for a moment and saw the door open a crack. This was odd to him as the cold weather got crueler by the hour. He felt no fear though, because he too knew a lord was with him, as the king told him. He thought he heard an angel whisper to him, "Come in."

He entered.

The bells of heaven called his name.

Pashmeira stood by the altar in the dimly lit church. A dark shadow moved about the church, and a row of pews to the left side of her were cast under a rainbow of soft silvery moonlight shining in through the stain glass windows. Her autumn garment no longer adorned her body. She was now clothed in her warmer midnight blue winter cloak. Her antlers twinkled soft blue dotted hues all around her while she watched the soldier posing as a friar walk into the sanctuary.

Underlin looked around, his eyes adjusting to the darkness. Pashmeira, breaking the silence, spoke. "The king has sent you to bring me back to him."

Underlin turned abruptly towards her voice and saw her. Her stain glass antlers delicately illuminated her face like a dove descending from the sky. He smiled a lustful smile. The witch was quite beautiful to his sight and aroused his desire. He hadn't lay with a woman in many moons. He decided he would take her first for himself and his pleasure before bringing her back to the king. Mockingly, he asked her, "Where is your mighty owl? You think he is your protector, but he cannot save you from my siege." Underlin spoke in a foreign tongue, but Pashmeira, the witch, could understand him, for that was one of her gifts.

Pashmeira replied, "He has gone back to his home in the great oak to tend to his parliament. He is not here, and you glorify only yourself in the tongue you speak."

Underlin, surprised she understood what he'd said, moved towards Pashmeira, looking at her closely. Her skin was beautiful, her hair was long and thick, and her lips were the color of wine. Studying the fitted garment on her body, he could surely see the shape of her figure underneath it. The garment would soon come off, he thought. Taking another step towards her, Underlin said in a foreign tongue, "I'm going to lay with you before I bring you to the king."

"This will not happen." Pashmeira stared at the soldier who forged the same path Mobley had, his fate already written in the stars. "You will not lay with me during your sojourn here, but you will be baptized by fire and spirit."

Underlin, the soldier, laughed and scoffed at her. What could she do to him? She could not stop him, this little woman with the fruitful body. He would take what he wanted. He moved another step closer to her.

Pashmeira moved not.

He leaned in, and his lips brushed along her face. She tasted like honey and salt. His beard tickled her cheek.

She smiled at him. He smelled like death to her.

He licked one side of her neck and then the other side. Pashmeira, the witch, moved not. Underlin kissed her sweet lips, and his arousal deepened.

Pashmeira's tongue touched his. "I would like to give you a gift," she said to the soldier posing as a friar.

"Do as you please, my beautiful lady," he said and smiled. He imagined the gift of her body. Would she take off her midnight robe?

Pashmeira walked to the entrance of the church and carefully took the winter wreath off the front door. She slowly carried it back and gently placed it on Underlin's head. He felt the sticks and sharp-pointed leaves poke into the flesh on his head. He queried, "What is this for?"

She spoke the words on her tongue, answering, "It is your crown of thorns, because you will suffer for your king."

Underlin heard a growl out of the darkness of the church from Warlawrn, the big black beast of a wolf with a white fire patch of fur on his chest and stardust blue eyes. He was sitting under the rainbow arch from the stain glass windows. One eye turned black and Warlawrn jumped off the pew he'd been resting on, pouncing on Underlin. The impact pushed Underlin's mouth onto the witch's garment. Underlin's tongue caught fire from the garment. He shouted in agony, flailing around trying to put out the fire, but the spirit of the fire proved to be stronger than him. The flames on his tongue shot up, catching the winter wreath on fire. Warlawrn attacked him again, this time knocking him down to the ground with dominant force—while his head burned and turned to ash.

With Underlin's throat and chest torn open, the wolf howled for his pack. They circled minutes later, eating the altar sacrifice.

PASHMEIRA, THE WITCH HELPS WARLAWRN, THE WOLF

In the days after Underlin's demise, Warlawrn continued to hunt with his pack. The snow lay deep on the ground, and his frosty paw prints impaled the ice. They picked up a few rabbits down in the ditch, but that was a measly little meal for him and his pack.

A wishing well sat at the cleft of the ditch where the fox and the hare bid each other farewell. He remembered when he'd first met Pashmeira years earlier. She drew water while he quietly came up behind her. She turned away from the well and saw him drooling. A conversation took place about what Warlawrn could do to Pashmeira. Then, the sun shined through her antlers and a rainbow of light cast upon Warlawrn's fur. His eyes turned from black to blue, and Pashmeira knew he would not harm her. Warlawrn appeared as the answer to her wish. In her lonely heartache of exile, she tossed a gold coin into the well just before he approached her. As the coin fell into the well, she made a magic wish. The coin plunked into the dark water at the bottom of the well and rippled a sad echo.

She wished for a friend, as true and strong as the wind, with a spirit that would never leave her. Warlawrn would be that friend, on one condition. He told Pashmeira she needed to help him through the winters of his life.

As Warlawrn hunted by the ditch in the years to follow, he never forgot the pact he made with Pashmeira, the witch by the well. Pashmeira helped Warlawrn through the winters, making sure he didn't starve. But Warlawrn the wolf wasn't Pashmeira pet, she was his.

He led the way further down the frozen river, deeper into the forest in search of deer and moose. One moose left tracks, indicating a weak leg. That moose proved to be a feast for the pack, but on a second attempt a few days later, the prey ran faster than the pack. Another winter storm blew into the forest of the fallen. The storm hit the earth so hard no animal could hunt, and no creature of prey could be about. The snow sang out, and the wind harmonized around everything, bringing a deep freeze with it. It became an unbearable tune. The pack retreated into their cave for a day to get past the worst part of the snowstorm. Shivering and hungry, they waited for it to pass. The next day Warlawrn decided to go out on his own, the conditions being too dangerous for the rest of his pack, especially his pups.

He traveled back up the riverbank towards the church. Along the way, Warlawrn encountered another pack of wolves who moved into his territory in search of food. He growled a warning to the other wolves. They didn't heed the warning and circled him. Warlawrn, never fearing a fight, leaped straight for the leader of their pack. He took him down in an instant, but the other wolves were at his back. He felt a sharp bite at his back leg, and at that moment, Orlawn swooped down and gouged out that wolf's eyes before he could bite again. The wolves, with their sight, ran away quickly. Warlawrn's leg bled into the snow, turning it from white to crimson.

In that moment, Orlawn appeared to Pashmeira, the witch in a vision, and she saw an injured Warlawrn. Gathering some clean cloths and an ointment, she ventured out to where they were, finding them quickly and tending to Warlawrn's wound. She gently rubbed the ointment on it and wound bandages around his leg. He limped back to the church with her, and Orlawn headed back to his oak tree to protect to his parliament. On the way, he caught two mice he heard moving underground. It wasn't much, but it would help.

Once back inside the warmth of the church, Pashmeira sat on a pew next to Warlawrn. She pet him gently and spoke softly to him, calming him. He fell asleep in her arms. The witch covered him with a blanket, and he slept for hours. Each year, the winter fell harder and harder on Warlawrn as he got older. His loyalty to his pack knew no bounds. He loved his pack, but he also needed the shelter and love the witch provided him. He took care of his pack, and the witch took care of Warlawrn.

"I cannot let my pack see me weak," Warlawrn said to the witch. She fed him some wolf chow, a blend of dried salmon, dried meat, and grains. Warlawrn promised the witch, "No matter how bad the winter gets, I will not eat you. I will never turn on you."

Pashmeira thought about this and said to him, "You could devour me in just a few minutes."

Warlawrn rested his head on her lap and replied, "I said I would not eat you, not that I could not eat you."

Pashmeira continued to pet him, and they kept each other warm that night, side by side on the old wooden church pew, under the blanket of leaves spun together with gold thread. Winter moonlight shined bright through the stain glass windows. The dove high atop a mountain lit up, like the heavens it was sent from.

The Threat of Winter Famine

Warlawrn's leg healed up in a few days, and Pashmeira fed him more wolf chow. He ate from her hand and licked her fingers clean. One day, she cooked him an egg because he was such a good boy. When Warlawrn spotted a flash of gray and smelled rodent, Pashmeira forbade him from eating the mouse. Monstros breathed a sigh of relief from the hole he'd been fearfully hiding in. Instead, she suggested he take a kettleful of wolf chow back to his pack. He wanted to keep it, and her, all for himself. Pashmeira told Warlawrn if his she-wolf found out he kept the wolf chow all for himself, she'd surely do him in. She scratched Warlawrn behind his ears and under his chin, insisting he take the kettleful back to his pack. He did. The pack ate the chow quickly, and this sustained them until their next kill.

Bertchwald slept peacefully in his cave on top of a mountain with his family. He dreamt of honey and honey cakes sprinkled with cinnamon. The witch made divine honey cakes for him in the spring. Bertchwald dreamt he ate stacks and stacks of honey cakes in a sunny meadow bathing in a gentle stream afterward.

His cubs slept next to him, staying nice and warm. His lady bear slept nestled on his other side. The winter sound of their continuous rhythmic snores echoed through the stone cave.

Orlawn spent most of his time in the great oak tree with his parliament. They discussed the wisdom of the forest planning for the future. Occasionally, he mated with his female owl. Sometimes, when they flew in the air, they locked talons and twirled around in circles together in the sky. The heavens opened for them when they mated. It was nature, and it was good.

Periodically, Orlawn flew to the king's castle. He circled it, and his ears picked up any sound from inside the castle. Orlawn flew around the watchtower several times. He heard the king say he knew Underlin must have died because he never came back. He would wait until the spring and send half his army into the forest of the fallen to bring the witch back to him. "Surely that pagan is no match for half my army," the king said.

During the rest of winter, the king sent his riotous army out into the town at night. Under the secrecy of darkness, they took what valuables and food they wanted from the townspeople. These revenues were the tax the king forced them to pay. When night fall came, the king got rich, very rich. The army was also instructed to bring the king back five more new wives. Winter bored him, and wife after wife kept the king warm and entertained through the winter solstice. The king told each one he loved them the most.

Warlawrn and his pack hunted for food. The near famine kept them alert and on the verge of a frenzy. A killing frenzy would take place soon. If a winter famine got bad enough, their thinking would be altered. Warlawrn's concern and hunger led him back to the witch. She gave him rest in the warm church, letting him sleep on the pew under a blanket of leaves. She gave him affection, petting him endlessly, and fed him wolf chow out of her hand to satisfy his hunger.

In the morning when they woke, the winter sun beamed through the stain glass windows of the church and down onto the pews. Through etched images of the saints in a boat on the Sea of Galilee, long streaks of vibrantly colored light covered Warlawrn and Pashmeira. They were drenched in a rainbow, a covenant of color encompassing them.

Pashmeira told Warlawrn to bring his she-wolf to her. "I will satisfy her hunger too and help strengthen her so that you may hunt again," she said. Warlawrn brought his she-wolf to Pashmeira, and Pashmeira fed the cold shaking she-wolf a handful of the wolf chow. The she-wolf grew very thin from the winter, and Pashmeira could see this through her thick fur coat. The she-wolf ate every speck of the wolf chow and looked at Pashmeira, wanting more.

Pashmeira fed her again with one hand, and with her other hand, she fed Warlawrn some. Both wolves ate out of Pashmeira's hands, licking them clean. They ate as much as they could until their hunger subsided. Like manna from heaven, the wolf chow never seemed to run out.

Pashmeira pet Warlawrn's she-wolf lulling the she-wolf to fall asleep. She covered her with a leaf blanket. The rest did the she-wolf good, as she was fatigued from the winter famine, too. She and Warlawrn were going to need to hunt again soon.

The next morning, Warlawrn and his she-wolf journeyed back out into the forest of the fallen to lead the hunt with their pack, but before they did, they stopped under a tall tree. Warlawrn danced a mating dance with his she-wolf. It was nature, and nature was good. They killed three foxes that day while the foxes were hunting for mice under the blanket of winter snow.

The sun peeked out briefly, and Pashmeira put on an old pair of gloves and ventured outside. The blanket of snow covering everything gave winter silence. Invigorated by cold fresh air, she scooped up some snow, making a snowman decorating him with twigs, stones, and an oak's acorns. She looked at him and smiled. In the middle of the bleakest time of year, she found a glimmer of joy.

While gazing at her man made of snow, amidst the joy, Pashmeira's eyes turned black. The rocks on the snowman spoke to her, and they told the tale of the king's boots walking over them and the parishioners being slaughtered.

A soldier had asked the king, "Shall we burn them, your majesty?"

King Kurlbach answered, "No. Bury them one by one and number the graves to tally with my other victories."

After this vision, Pashmeira removed the glove from her right hand. She placed her palm on the snowman's head. The heat from her fury melted the ice. From the puddle of water, she cupped some in her hands, pouring it over her head; she baptized herself in anger over the injustice.

THE SACRIFICIAL SON

Winter dipped much colder and oppressed the land day and night. There was no prey to be had. Hungry and shivering, Warlawrn looked up into the evening sky. The stars shined bright that night. He watched two stars collide; glimmering starbursts speckled the sky. He knew what he had to do. He gathered his pack, and they traveled out of the forest of the fallen to the kingdom bridge. Surely a pig would be eating in a trough, he thought. Weak and starving, he led the way across the old wooden bridge, paws thumping along. His pups followed behind him, and his she-wolf brought up the back.

A winter plague attacked the kingdom, taking many lives. It brought a cough to the lungs and a fever to the skin. Anyone who died from it was forbidden to be buried in the kingdom for fear the plague would continue to spread. The king lost four of his wives and two of his daughters to the plague. He knew this was the witch's doing, and he vowed to himself to end her evil life.

That same dark night, the king sent some of his soldiers out into the town to take him more wealth and wives. One family with a beautiful flax haired daughter just of age did not want her to go. She was the favorite of her father, a father who knew how evil the king was. On chance for a peaceful surrender, the soldier said to her father, "We will take her either way."

Courageously, the father replied, "You will take her over my spilled blood." And they did... along with a small bag of copper coins and two loaves of bread.

The soldiers invaded the next cottage over, only to find a piece of dried fish and a golden vase on the fireplace hearth. The king's soldiers confiscated all.

In the midnight hour, Warlawrn led the wolf pack into town. Roaming around, he spotted a chicken coop. The rooster crowed, signaling not that light was near, but that darkness was upon them. Predators were amidst, and the cock warned the chicks:

**"Cock-a-doodle-doo!
The wolves have come to eat you!"**

The rooster's crowing alerted the king's soldiers something was amiss. Seeing the soldier in the distance, Warlawrn led his pack away from the coop and further into the town, smelling opossum stew bubbling in a pot over a fire. He traveled towards the aroma, his pups scampering behind him. The door to the old woman's cottage had a crack in it. Warlawrn peered through it. Seeing the stew, he pushed on the door, entering the home. The lady of the house, not wanting to give up her meal, shooed Warlawrn away. Her broom swatting at him, he growled a warning to her. Crazed with hunger, Warlawrn pounced on her and bit her throat. His she-wolf knocked the pot over and the pack ate quickly. The lady's family heard the commotion and rushed to see what happened. Their screaming brought the soldiers to their home.

In a few moments passing, the king's soldiers appeared in the doorway. They drew swords, and Warlawrn and his she-wolf tried to fight, but the soldiers outnumbered them. Warlawrn held them off while his she-wolf jumped through their window. The pups followed, but in the commotion, one pup was cut with the sword. Warlawrn, hearing the yelp, turned to see his son slain.

One of Warlawrn's blue eyes turned black, and he attacked faster than a lightning bolt. Warlawrn bit the hand of the slaying soldier, ripping it off. The soldier cried out in agony—blood flowing everywhere. Warlawrn picked his pup up in his mouth and jumped through the window before the other soldiers could get to him, running as fast as he could to catch up to his pack.

They made it safely across the bridge and walked gravely back to their sleeping place. That cold winter night, they buried their pup and mourned. With broken hearts, Warlawrn and his she-wolf vowed to kill any soldier they could to avenge their beloved son.

The news made it back to Orlawn the same night. His parliament discussed this in their old oak tree. "This winter is the worst one we've had," Orlawn said.

"What can we do?" another owl asked.

"I know where a sly fox lives. I will tell Warlawrn of his whereabouts," Orlawn replied. In the morning, Orlawn flew to Warlawrn in the winter sun. He informed him, "The fox, a large old one, lives by the three pines down at the frozen creek, next to the cluster of dwarf evergreens. He has a tiny cave in an oval stone. You will find him there."

Warlawrn led his family out to the frozen creek. The old fox lay in a snow patch by the frozen creek. His fur and eyes were the color of amber, and his tail was tipped with black. A white fury stomach kept him warm in the winter. Snowflakes trickled down on the fox and rested upon his fiery colored fur. Hearing the wolf's paws coming, the fox stood and shook the snowflakes off him. He hurried into his oval rock cave to hide.

The wolves dug out his hiding place. The fox, with nowhere to run, gave them their meal that day.

PASHMEIRA'S DREAM

The old church grew colder, but not as cold as the forest. The wood pile Pashmeira stored up dwindled smaller each day. She put ground apple seeds in her tea and sat by the fire. The hearth around the fireplace stayed warm and glowed with light. The days were short, and the nights were long. Solitude comforted her for a while, but she knew the king would send his army as soon as spring came. She wove a scarf with her gold thread to pass the time and meditated on the wisdom of the earth.

Some days, she climbed up the old creaky wooden steps in the church to the attic and sat on a ledge by a tiny round window. Monstros scampered along the windowsill, and she fed him pumpkin seeds. One particularly cold day, she made a warm bed for Monstros out of a giant empty eggshell. He curled up and took a long, peaceful winter nap.

As Monstros slept, Pashmeira peered out the tiny window in the drafty church attic. Frost dusted pines were all she could see in between a blanket of pure white snow, covering the entire forest of the fallen. The howling wind broke the silence. She wondered what her friends were doing. Opening the window, she placed seven dried pomegranate seeds on a shallow silver dish sitting on the windowsill. In the distance, she heard the caw, caw, caw.

Atop a patch of snow on the castle wall, perched Crueneilious the crow, dark gray claws crunching into the ice. His beady black eyes spotted a key hanging on a hook, and next to the key, a soldier stood guard of the kingdom's castle. The soldier shivered on that cold winter day. Not being able to tolerate the chill in the wind any longer, he took refuge in an alcove and fell asleep. During the soldier's slumber, Crueneilious plucked the key off the hook, promptly flying it back to Pashmeira at the old abandoned church.

Crueneilious landed on the windowsill and dropped the key to the kingdom's castle next to the silver dish and ate his pomegranate seeds.

"Thank you, my love," Pashmeira said, surveying the key to the castle and remembering her first encounter with the king.

To spurn his advances almost meant death for her. She remembered how he beat her and the look of enjoyment on his lascivious face while he beat her. Had she not been clothed in her garment; he would have taken her life. She thought of Warlawrn, Orlawn and Bertchwald. She missed them all, but their spirits stayed in her heart, giving her peace.

Winter continued to dominate the earth for many more days, and Warlawrn couldn't stay away from the witch. The winter proved to be the worst one yet, and he needed more wolf chow. He needed rest. He needed to hear Pashmeira's voice. Her voice sounded sweet and lovely to his ears. He came back by himself several more times, bringing her gifts of daffodils he plucked from snow patches with his teeth, setting them at Pashmeira's feet, wagging his tail.

They lay by the fire together, and she dusted snowflakes off his whiskers. He said, "The deer and moose tracks have not been easy to find. The winter trail is dead."

Pashmeira stroked him and said, "If you cannot hunt from above the snow, you will need to go under the snow. Hunt like the fox."

Warlawrn replied, "I'd rather eat the fox."

The next morning, she sent Warlawrn away with a kettleful of wolf chow for him and his pack. She warned him not to be greedy and keep it to himself. He promised he wouldn't.

Alone again, Pashmeira lay in her bed. She slept a deep sleep and while she did, Orlawn appeared to her in a dream. She stood at the bottom of his great oak tree and looked up at him perched on it. In the dream, he said, "Half the king's army will come for you soon, but do not fear."

Pashmeira asked him, "Why should I not be afraid? I have only a distant owl, an old wolf and a hungry, sleeping honey bear to look after me."

Orlawn replied, "You have not been hurt thus far." He flew from his great oak and circled the forest in the cold air, watching everything. Pashmeira dreamt a rainbow appeared over the forest and kingdom, catching fire, and dripping onto everything.

To the Cave

When Pashmeira woke the next morning, her bones felt heavy, and her heart hurt. She knew her communion with winter would be over soon, and it wouldn't be long before the king sent his army for her. In fact, the king had already given instructions to his army. When the river thawed, they were to sail down it and bring her back. They were warned not to touch her garment. They were to take a chain with them and place that around her neck and treat her like the evil dogs she ran with.

In the days to follow, Pashmeira's hand branch broom swept the church clean and stacked logs on the fire, keeping it burning. Pashmeira contemplated the future. Her Lord imparted wisdom to her. Picking up an owl quill pen, she began writing. The stain of the ink on the parchment told the tale of the seasons to come. She melted wax, dripping it onto the scroll. Drop by drop, the hot red waxy liquid stained the paper like blood. She took out the compass from her pocket, and by stamping the wax with the top of the ornately carved compass, the fate of King Kurlbach and Pashmeira was sealed.

Warlawrn was not with her, but his spirit surrounded her. He hunted and searched and searched and hunted. The days grew warmer, and the snow thawed a little more each day. Temperatures finally rose above freezing. Early one morning after Warlawrn and his pack took down a large moose and devoured it, he peered out at the river. The water flowed again, and a bright morning star shined high above the river in the middle of the lush, green forest. Like a game of chess, the king had made his next move.

Warlawrn gazed at the beautiful river run and spotted the boats with half the king's army in them. Warlawrn outran the wind. He had to get to Pashmeira before those boats touched the river's shore. His paws dug into the patches of melting snow as he went down along the riverbank to the church. He panted and ran and ran and panted. He pushed through the church door and saw Pashmeira standing under the stain glass window. She was barely visible, as her antlers blended in with the images on the windows of a vibrant blue sky with pink ribbons of swirly clouds.

"We must go now!" he beckoned her with panting breath.

Pashmeira gathered up her golden scarf, her broom, a bag of grains, a skull cup, the key to the castle, and her scroll. She blew out the candles and said farewell to Monstros by picking him up and taking him outside the front door, setting him free from what would happen next. Squeaking, he ran in circles fearfully.

They set out in haste, exiting through the back door of the old church and down the stone steps to the river. A tiny wooden boat with two oars awaited them. Pashmeira and Warlawrn climbed into the boat quickly, and she paddled furiously. Warlawrn helped to paddle with his paw. They sailed further west, downstream and around some mountains. The army sailed from the north to the south. Pashmeira and Warlawrn were south of the kingdom and sailing further west.

When the army arrived at the abandoned church, they found it had been swept clean and the witch was not there. They lit the church on fire. Flames ignited the old wooden church pews, parishioner seats turned to ash. Inside the church, it grew so hot the colors on the stain glass windows melted. The faces of the saints in the windows grew long and horrified looking. The stain glass windows cracked and popped, shattering colored pieces of glass everywhere. Vivid melting glass shined brightly all over the ground, and the wooden roof caved in, and the stone walls charred black. The trees around the church caught fire. Monstros looked on in horror and scurried behind a cluster of rocks to hide, gray fur shaking.

Pashmeira and Warlawrn sailed down around the other side of the river shore by the mountains. Looking up revealed nothing but smoke in a fire sky with an orange sun. Out of the smoke flew Orlawn with his wings outspread, soaring through the clouds of ashy mist. His right talon held Pashmeira's gold and copper compass. She left it behind, but he retrieved it. Swooping down, landing in front of Pashmeira and Warlawrn, he gave the compass to Pashmeira and said, "Use this whenever you feel lost. The king's army went east. You are safe for now."

Swirls of patina covered the magic copper compass, and Pashmeira looked at it, watching the cloudy ancient film on it twist and turn. Out of the green clouds burst an image of a lion seated on a throne. She stared into the lion's eyes, and an emerald rainbow encircled him. Pashmeira saw his eyes and the rainbow catch fire. From the flames rode a white horse with a crown. She heard the rumble and peals of thunder.

She opened the compass lined with gold on the inside, and a rainbow of light beamed covering her and Warlawrn. It pointed them north-west, and so they went the way of the compass, further into the mountain range. A flash of lightning exploded across the sky.

Pashmeira and Warlawrn traveled as fast as they could through the deep forest and up the mountain that led to Bertchwald's den. Orlawn circled in the air high above them, keeping watch through the smoke. Their steps were many as they went. They finally approached the top of the mountain at sunset, the sky still burned bright orange from the church forest fire.

Warlawrn spoke, "They have destroyed the house of the Lord."

"Our God is still with us," Pashmeira said, receiving a vision of graves being dug for the soldiers. "If that army were to ignite, I would not cry one tear to extinguish the flames."

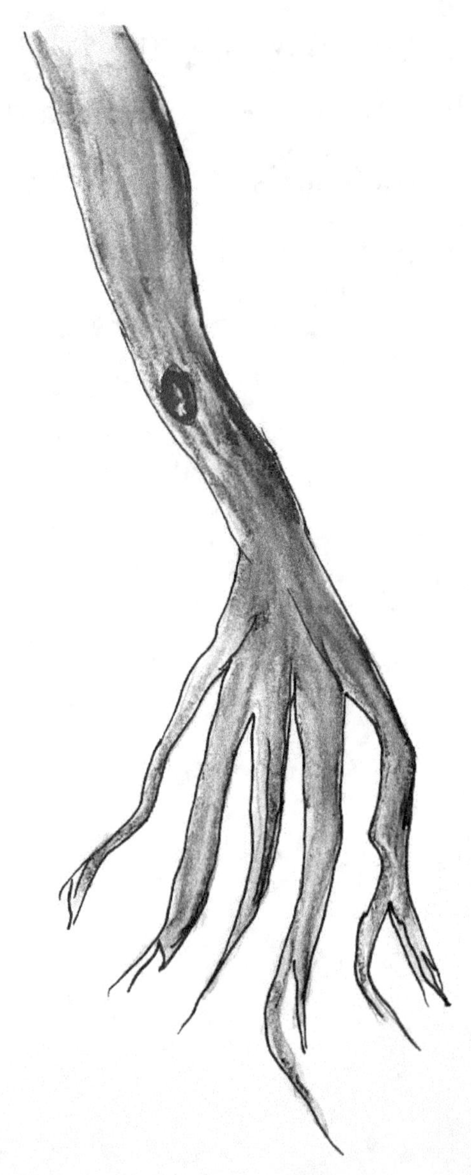

The Bear's Spring Awakening

The Bear

Bertchwald was the bear, and oh, what a sacrificial bear he was!

The spring belonged to him

right after hibernation made him a little thin.

He mated and hibernated

and hibernated and mated.

Every winter kept him snoozing in a cave,

while other animals met their grave.

When spring sprung him out of his hibernation,

he would lay in the fields of flowers

for hours.

A honey bear was Bertchwald.

Oh, with the honey he was enthralled.

A drizzle of honey on his chin,

gave him quite a grin.

His candy makers were the bumblebees,

and he'd shake their hives right out of the trees.

He thought about honey day and night.

He'd search high and low until he got it in his sight.

Chunks of honeycomb made him moan with delight.

The honey would drip from his claws, making all kinds of nature stick to his paws.

But even Bertchwald could not live on honey alone.

He'd travel upstream to find him some fish on the bone.

His sharp, black claws speared so much salmon,

his family would never know a famine.

He was the fastest fisher in the stream,

but he could also be mean.

He was a dutiful father,

and with his cubs and lady bear, you'd better not bother.

When you find him sleeping and not woke,

don't, whatever you do, DON'T give him a poke!

If he growls, you better run

before his growl bursts your eardrum.

The butterflies will scatter.

The little rabbit's feet will pitter patter

away to a safe place,

away from his angry face.

When the bear met the witch in a flower field, she interrupted his slumber.

The wind rattled with his roar and almost did her under.

"How dare you disturb me from my sleep," the bear said to the witch,

to which the witch replied, "I know where the honey is."

The bear was obsessed with the witch ever since,

and so, with his claws, her flesh, he would never mince.

No matter how many times she woke him,
and the angry roars and mood that fell foul,
his face could only scowl
and his throat could only growl.
He could not, he would not, strike her down,
because he wanted only honey thick to dribble down his chin.
Sweet golden honey...
on a beautiful day shining sunny.

Bertchwald the Bear Awakens

With still quite a chill in the air, Bertchwald, his lady bear, and his cubs continued to sleep their deep hibernation of peace and renewal. The rhythm of their snores created a symphony of slumber inside the orchestra of their cave, warm with bear's body heat. Pashmeira, the witch and Warlawrn, the wolf stood at the edge of Bertchwald's cavernous home, cold and tired.

Looking into the dark rock tunnel, Warlawrn said, "We dare not wake him."

Pashmeira's broom scratched at the ground, sweeping up a mound of fallen leaves. She and Warlawrn needed rest from their travels that day. They laid down next to each other on the leaves, nestled in, and slept side by side, keeping each other warm at the edge of Bertchwald's cave.

The next morning, the air smelled of smoke, and ash floated through the sky like dead snowflakes blowing out of a storm of burning worship. Pashmeira knew the king's army would search the entire forest for her. Her great big bear protector slept deeply while part of her forest church shelter had burned to the ground. Orlawn flew back to his parliament and perched on his great oak, keeping watch over the forest of the fallen.

After another day of waiting for Bertchwald to wake, Warlawrn told Pashmeira, "I must go back to my pack soon. I must lead the hunt again for them. My spirit will be with you. Do not fear."

Pashmeira scratched him behind his ears and under his chin. Warlawrn put his paw in her hand, and Pashmeira caressed it and said a sad goodbye to him.

On Warlawrn's way back down the mountain, he sniffed the scent of a deer and traced it to find her all alone. He hadn't eaten in a day. She was a beautiful little doe, with big glassy eyes looking out in timid fear from the sides of her head. Golden brown fur with white speckled spots dotted her back. A fluffy pelt on her soft under belly waited to be ripped open. She arched her neck back and nibbled gently on a few new green leaves that dangled from a low-hanging branch of a tree. Warlawrn watched her for a few minutes, his hunger growing as he did. As the timid doe quietly nibbled on the leaves, the fragrance of them permeated her nostrils. The first sunbeams of spring shined pushing winter out.

Warlawrn waited a few more minutes and let her continue to eat the leaves... her last meal. That tiny doe never saw Warlawrn coming.

After the kill, Warlawrn traveled back down the mountain, and Pashmeira stayed at Bertchwald's cave, waiting another day with the weather warming to well above freezing. Finding silkworms spinning silk fibers, Pashmeira spent the next two days weaving those fibers into fabric, dyeing the fabric the bright color of the poppies from a field next to Bertchwald's cave. Once the fabric had dried, she shed her winter cloak. Her autumn garment had been left behind as well, for that season in her life came to a fiery end.

She fashioned a new silky gown, tying her gold scarf around her waist like a sash. The gown fluttered in the gentle wind. She captured the rays of sunshine and spun more gold, making a pair of sandals. Some daisies grew out of the ground by the cave, and she picked them, fastening them in her long flame-like hair lining the edges of her stain glass antlers. That day, the antlers shined bright yellow like the spring sun. Even with half the king's army searching for her in the east, gratefulness filled her heart for the beautiful earth she stood on, and the Spirit who guided her through it.

Another day went by. The next morning, the birds chirped early as if to say, "Spring is here!" Pashmeira descended the mountain, searching the land. She heard a buzzing noise not too far off. She followed the noise to its source, passing some rocks with a dove's nest hiding in between the cracks. The soft sound of the dove cooing soothed her. She strolled along until she came to a tree housing a new beehive hanging from its lowest branch and smiled. Throwing her broom up at it in one motion, the hand of the broom grabbed the beehive down from its branch and flew back towards Bertchwald's cave with it. Surely, the smell of honey would wake him, the witch thought.

Following the broom back, she noticed the patches of snow on the ground were melting away and were much smaller. Blades of green grass sprang up through the snow patches and cut through winter. New blooming flowers sprouted everywhere. Some purple flowers caught her eye. Upon closer inspection, she found them to be wild lavender and picked a few to take them to the cave with her, tucking them in the sash of her spring garment.

Once back at the bear's den, she gathered a bundle of wood to start a fire. Vigorously rubbing two sticks, she got a flame to catch and stoked it. She mixed some honey and lavender with a bit of the grains in her bag, placing the sticky mixture on the end of a branch. Holding it over the fire for several minutes, she turned it every so often to keep it from burning. This honey cake would surely wake the bear, the witch thought.

It did not.

She made another one and waited again. Bertchwald did not wake, but dreamt of sweet, sweet honey cakes in his mouth.

Pashmeira decided to poke the bear. She set the honey cakes down on a large rock and picked up her broom. She tiptoed over to Bertchwald and gently poked him with the handle end of the broom. His snores were loud, like a trumpet. She gently poked him again. He continued to snore. She gently poked him again. He continued to snore. She flipped the broom around and dropped it on the bear, hand end of the broom side down. The hand of the broom promptly smacked Bertchwald across his sleeping face.

The cave shook from his roar, and the mountain trembled underneath them.

Pashmeira, the Witch Follows Bertchwald, the Bear

Bertchwald roared so loud, Orlawn heard him from his great oak tree a few mountains north as he kept watch over the forest. Bertchwald roared so loud, Warlawrn heard him from the bottom of the mountain and down the riverbank. With the gold scarf in her hand, Pashmeira waved it back and forth over the honey cakes towards Bertchwald, the growling bear. The second he got a whiff of the honey cakes; he stopped roaring and sniffed the air. He sniffed and sniffed and sniffed at the sweet smell of the warm honey cakes.

Slowly Bertchwald got up from the earth he hibernated on for months. The ground knew the shape of his body and had given way to it. Bertchwald stepped out of that crevice and stretched, moving his neck around. He grunted and reared up on his hind legs and rubbed his back against the rocky wall of the cave. Yawning, he scratched himself with his big black claws. He tottered over to Pashmeira. Saliva dripped from his sharp, jagged teeth. He devoured every speck of a honey cake out of the witch's hand, looking at her for more. She fed him another.

Pashmeira informed him, "While you were sleeping, the king sent a second fake friar to find me and bring me back to him. Warlawrn and his pack ate him. Then, the king sent half his army into the forest to find me. Warlawrn and Orlawn guided me here before the king's army burned down the church and part of the forest. They look for me now in the southeast."

"Good thing we are in the northwest. Now, I'm hungry and must get myself some salmon. A bear cannot live on honey cakes alone."

Pashmeira followed him down the mountain to the crystal blue stream overflowing with wild salmon. Along the way, the flowers sang out and sprung up all over the ground. The wind made the flowers dance, and the birds serenaded them. The sun shined warm through the crisp air. A merry march traveled them downhill. The sound of the flowing river grew louder and louder as they descended. They first passed the oval-shaped river tucked in between a circle of mountains and trees. Pashmeira stopped, and Bertchwald said, "No, we must go upstream a bit. That's where all the action is."

Pashmeira followed Bertchwald through the lush green mossy patches and trees and rocks. Mists of water sprayed everywhere from racing water, hitting the rocks along the stream. This was of no bother to Bertchwald, as his coat was rather thick, and the water didn't penetrate his fur. He stayed nice and warm while Pashmeira's spring garment got drenched, and she shivered in her cold skin. She pressed upstream until they got to just the right spot.

A rapidly running stream overflowed with salmon. Salmon jumped around and swam back and forth. Bertchwald smiled. It was all his for the taking. He waded in knee deep and watched the pretty fish swim. Their slippery skin glistened in the sun. He opened his mouth, and one flew right in as it tried to swim upstream. Bertchwald gulped it and went in for more. He ate and hunted and hunted and ate until his belly was stuffed full. With his black knife-like claws, he speared several more. He'd take them home to his family. Untying the gold scarf Pashmeira had tied around her waist as a sash, she placed the fish in it to carry them back. Bertchwald caught so many fish he never noticed when Pashmeira took a few to dry to make sure Warlawrn never went hungry. Warlawrn stayed in Pashmeira's heart and mind no matter where she went. The wind of Warlawrn's spirit rustled her hair, and he dwelled in her heart on that soft spring day, giving her hope. Blooming flowers whispered sweet nothings in her ear. For spring is the season everything awakens, covering the earth with rebirth.

GONE FISHING

Instead of going back the way they came, Bertchwald, the bear, insisted on going up the other side of the mountain to get back to his cave. He said this would be easier. It was not. When they walked around the other side of the mountain and through a field of flowers, she trailed behind him, carrying his heavy load of salmon for his family. Bertchwald marched much slower now. In fact, he came to a complete stop and said to the witch, "You'll need to excuse me for a few minutes."

And Pashmeira would never ever need to ask the age-old question 'does a bear shit in the woods?' because that day she found out.

Once done, Bertchwald needed a nap. It had been three months since he'd been able to nap in a sunny field of flowers. It was the loveliest thing a bear could do. He rolled around and settled in. Hours of sleeping brought him more dreams of honeycomb in this field of fresh spring flowers.

Pashmeira thought it would be unwise of her to sit out in an open field when half the king's army was in search of her. She trudged her way into a thicket of trees and sat down on a huge rock. Looking up into the sky, she saw Orlawn circling above, keeping watch on his way to survey the kingdom. She rested her back on the trunk of a giant tree and waited for Bertchwald to finish his nap. Her time was of no concern to Bertchwald, nor was her aching back from carrying his load of fish. He was the mighty salmon hunter, and like the sun, he led the way for his family to greener pastures. At times, he would make them lie down with him and rest amongst the daisies and poppies.

Pashmeira closed her eyes and Warlawrn's spirit comforted her. She wondered what he was doing, and she knew the warmer weather would be easier on him. Since spring had sprung, Warlawrn and his pack went on a bit of a killing spree. The winter famine affected them gravely. They'd all lost weight and felt weaker than normal. They were hungry, and it was time to kill again. Foxes, deer, rabbits, elks. It was all theirs for the taking now, too. Warlawrn led the way for their hunts. On instinct, they killed more than they could eat. One day, they even made their way over to a shepherd's field in the neighboring town and killed every single sheep, leaving only a few bones and some tufts of wool behind.

Orlawn, on the other hand, was more concerned with saving lives. In the new spring weather, he left his parliament and flew over the kingdom. He circled the king's palace many times to find out what was going on there. The king added to his superfluity of wives by having his soldiers bring ten more virgins to the king to marry. A few of his former wives met the guillotine for behaviors found unacceptable to the king.

When some of his wives grew tired of the lack of attention from him, they decided they could please each other without the king. While the thought of his wives pleasing each other pleased the king, these wives had not been granted permission from the king to engage in such a behavior without him. Their executions were justified by order of law, and their headless bodies joined the forest of the fallen. The law of the land stated all **F**ornication must be **U**nder the **C**onsent of the **K**ing. That was the decree he put in place several years back. After all, that is where the word came from.

The king also prepared for his summer circus. They were employing jugglers, clowns, and lion tamers from all over different parts of the land. It proved difficult to find a good lion tamer. A man who did not fear the creatures that could swiftly end his life was rare. In turn, the ringmaster was quite easy to find. The king simply searched for a man with the most grandiose demeanor, expelling hot air everywhere.

The king imported some lions and tigers from a far-off country. He procured elephants, camels, zebras, giraffes, monkeys, and horses. New tents were being constructed, and the bearded lady told not to shave. A fearless, agile tightrope walker would be a star act. Horror seized her mind when she found out the king would not allow a net. "What fun would that be?" the king asked. Her broken bones were of no concern to him.

This would be another magnificent event to celebrate his mighty kingdom. It would not pay for itself, though, and the people of the king's land were taxed heavily to pay for this lofty event. Some of them were forced to give up what little they owned for the event they were forbidden to attend, which was also of no concern to the king.

LES LOUPS ET LES BREBIS.

In Search of the Sweet, Sweet Honey

Pashmeira grew tired of waiting for Bertchwald to wake from his nap. She breathed in deep, looking up at the tree she sat with her back against. Peering up at the trunk, she noticed a tiny cocoon attached to the side of it. She stared at it for a few moments, witnessing the cocoon wiggling. The worm had turned. Its chrysalis castle would soon be no longer. The butterfly inside began to stretch and come to life. It struggled to get out. Pashmeira wondered if the struggle brought pain to the butterfly. In just that moment, the beautiful, winged creature emerged from the cocoon—a new creation!

Its wings, colored in yellow and orange, spread wide and fluttered through the air. How glorious a sight! Pashmeira longed to fly free with the butterflies, to be a new creation with a new life. Instead, she'd been exiled by an evil king out of the kingdom and now hid in the forest of the fallen, dodging a blood thirsty army.

Her broom picked a bouquet of spring flowers, flew to Pashmeira, and presented them to her. She took them in her hand

and moved from the rock she sat on, approaching Bertchwald, where he lay comfortably in the grassy field of spring flowers. Since she was still carrying the heavy load of fish in one hand and flowers in the other, she asked her broom to give Bertchwald a little poke. He woke from his afternoon nap growling at her so loud it almost cracked her eardrums.

She said, "I know where the honey is."

He stopped his roar and stood. She instructed him to follow her back up the mountain. She trekked along carrying his load of fish in her gold scarf as they hiked back up the mountain. Bertchwald reminded her, "If you find any honey along the way to the other honey, please let me know."

About halfway up the mountain, Pashmeira heard the buzzing. She followed the sound to the source, with Bertchwald salivating behind her. This time, the beehive formed in the hole of a tree stump. It appeared the tree had been knocked over in a storm and cracked in half. The half still in the ground housed this sticky sweet substance that Bertchwald could not get enough of. Honey made him want honey. More honey made him want even more honey. Bertchwald possessed an insatiable appetite for the honey.

Pashmeira stepped aside so Bertchwald could partake in it. Watching the bees swarm the hive protecting the queen and keeping her alive, she warned him, "You will get stung."

This did not stop Bertchwald, as he had to have the honey! He went in for it and pulled out an enormous chunk of honeycomb, bees swarming all around him. Bertchwald swatted at them, but they stung and stung and stung him through his thick fur and on his nose. Chewing on the honeycomb filled him with delight as they did. It stung so good. He reached in for more honey, and it dripped from his claws. Bertchwald ate every last speck of honey in that honeycomb. He did not save any for his family. When he was done, he looked at the witch and said, "I ache all over."

Pashmeira picked up some dirt in her hand, spiting on it to make mud. She spread the cold wet mud on Bertchwald's bee stings. This brought him relief.

The bear and the witch continued up the mountain after Bertchwald's honey fest. He stopped to scratch his back on a tree, and he thought it was time for another nap. He rolled around in a patch of grass and daisies settling in. Pashmeira waited for him patiently, still carrying his heavy load of fish for his family. Eventually, they made it to the top of the mountain and around the bend to his cave.

His lady bear and cubs were all awake now, happy to see him come home with the salmon. They thanked big bear daddy for all the salmon he brought back for them. A daisy stuck to the side of Bertchwald's honey sticky cheek. He picked it off, giving it to his lady bear. Fur friction between Bertchwald and his lady bear began a mating dance. They disappeared behind the cave. It was mating season, and it was good.

Pashmeira handed out fish from her gold scarf to all the cubs until they ate their fill. The cubs frolicked through fields of sun kissed flowers brimming with pollen. When the lady bear came back, she ate salmon from Pashmeira.

Night softly cloaked the day, and it was time to go back to the den. Pashmeira slept alone on her pile of leaves with a growling stomach. The family of bears ate all the salmon and did not leave any for her.

The next morning, Pashmeira woke first. Venturing out to the land at sunrise, she found a small measure of mulberries. She ate some of them and found some leaves to brew tea with. Back at the cave, she set seven berries on a shiny leaf for her little feathered friend, wondering what he was doing.

Caw, caw, caw.

On that sunny spring morning, several of the king's children scampered about the royal courtyard, happy winter had ended. Crueneilious, the crow perched himself on a long branch of a Maple tree watching the eldest children play a game of marbles. The children flicked the mibs, knocking them about; the winner cheering and the loser crying. At their mother's call, they scurried into the castle for morning porridge.

Crueneilious swooped down, picking up a cobalt blue marble swirled with tangerine-colored stripes glistening in the sun. Holding it tightly in his black beak, he flew the marble to Pashmeira at Bertchwald's cave. He dropped it at her feet and ate his measure of mulberries from the shiny smooth leaf.

"Thank you, my love," Pashmeira said, holding the marble up to the sunlight, admiring its beauty. With gift in pocket 'twas time to make a fire to boil water for her tea. She found two knotted sticks. While rubbing them together to start a fire, Pashmeira recited her witch's chant:

"Friction, friction, smoke, and fire,
Feel the heat burning your feet.
Raising up from the ground
raging flames consuming the earth abound
bringing you down, down
into the depths of hell.
For this reason, we cast a spell
to ignite the power
at the witching hour.
In us is a sword bearing spirit.
It's calling.
Do you hear it?"

Smoke emanated from the sticks, and a flame ignited. Pashmeira held the burning sticks to some dried brush and stoked the fire. Scooping up snow, icy gusts of air kissed her face, and she packed the snow into the skull of a fallen warrior. She boiled fragrant tea leaves in the water, and drank it by herself in the quiet moments of the morning, before the bear family woke up. When the cubs awoke, they tossed and tumbled rambunctiously.

Bertchwald insisted Pashmeira take his lady bear down to the special spot in the river to fish for more salmon for all of them. Pashmeira wove a fine new basket with a handle to hold the fish, and Pashmeira and Bertchwald's lady bear descended the mountain by themselves. They walked along the oval river circled by mountains and trees and up the riverbank to the special spot upstream. Again, the spray from the rapidly running water hit the rocks, making misty air rain down. The mist bounced off Bertchwald's lady bear and drenched Pashmeira and her brightly colored garment. They made their way to the special spot.

Once they arrived, his mate waded into the river knee deep. Now it was his mate's time to eat until she had her fill. The lady bear fished down into the water and speared a salmon with her claws. She ate the slippery gray skinned fish and speared another one. Reaching back into the water again and again, she even caught one in her back claw, flipping it in the air and catching it in her sharp mouth. Pashmeira watched Bertchwald's lady bear eat and eat and eat. The lady bear hunted and killed as ferociously as Bertchwald.

Once Bertchwald's lady bear ate her fill of salmon, she hunted for her family. Pashmeira stacked the extra salmon the lady bear caught in her basket until it filled up. She stood holding the basket at the edge of the river stream, and Bertchwald's lady bear pitched a few more wild salmon into it, topping the basket off. Pashmeira thought about getting a fish for herself. Her stomach growled with hunger.

While contemplating this, everything went black—a burlap sack flung over her head. Pashmeira struggled to get free. Burlap rubbed and burned against her face and neck. Her own hot breath trapped inside the bag against her face. Her antlers poked and caught on the burlap. Men laughed, and Pashmeira heard Bertchwald's lady bear's growl in the distance—roaring like thunder!

THE BATTLE CRY

The cold, heavy, thick chain constricted around Pashmeira's throat like a python choking the life out of its prey. She felt a tree scratching at her back, and she heard the men mocking her. They chained her to a tree like a dog and pulled the bag from her head. She stood face to face with the general of the army. He snarled at her. Unlike the real friar and the fake friar sent before him, this man did not have lust for her. This man possessed a lust for power and wanted to humiliate her, believing Pashmeira to be filth beneath his clean, sinless feet.

"The witch," he said, exposing rotten teeth in a mouth, speaking only hypocrisy.

He smelled like death to her, and she detested him. The general looked at the antlers on her head, and they did not shine for him but appeared as dead elk antlers.

He said to Pashmeira, "You think you are a wild animal with those ridiculous antlers resting on your skull? You cannot buck the king when he mounts you." As if on command, the army obediently laughed at the general's joke.

Pashmeira looked around, seeing many soldiers standing at attention, staring at her. Bertchwald's lady bear was gone. Pashmeira stood alone with half the king's army. The general turned to speak to his soldiers. "We will camp here tonight before bringing this witch back to the king."

The general ordered a few soldiers to cook the fish in the basket from the catch of the day. Pashmeira, the witch, remained chained to the tree as the men ate the salmon. The basket full of fish was enough to feed all the men. Once they were done with their meal, Pashmeira spoke to the general, "You must be tired from your travels through the forest in search of me. Please, let me wash your feet to refresh you."

This angered the general. Who was this witch to speak to him? He wondered. He stepped closer to her and said, "Your garment is wet. Perhaps we should take it off you first before you wash everyone's feet."

The army laughed with evil infected hearts.

At this remark, a brave, smart soldier spoke up, "General, the king said not to touch her garment."

The general nodded and spoke mockingly. "If this dirty heretic wants to wash our feet, who am I to stop her?"

The men laughed again, and the brave soldier unchained her from the tree, taking care not to touch her garment.

Pashmeira moved closer towards the general and stood face to face with him. "If you do not serve, you cannot lead."

The general scoffed, "I do not serve! I command!"

"Have you ever been persecuted for telling the truth?" Pashmeira wondered.

The general's eyes narrowed. "No one would dare persecute me."

"Sweet are the feet that bring good news. You do not speak the truth since you have not been persecuted." Pashmeira's antlers stood tall above them.

Pashmeira, the witch, collected a large branch that had been split down the middle from lightning, hallow like a tiny canoe. Slowly walking to the river, she filled the branch with clean water and walked back to the general, getting down on her knees in front of him. After untying the gold scarf from her waist, she dipped it in the water. She removed the general's sandals and wiped the general's feet with it, massaging his feet as she cleaned them. This relaxed the general, and he instructed her to wash the feet of his twelve majors, for they too were weary from their travels. One by one, Pashmeira, the witch, washed the feet, these men drawing a clean branch full of water each time. Some of them were so relaxed they fell asleep, and some of them thought she put them in a trance because they were too tired to move.

Bertchwald's lady bear had run back up the mountain and told Bertchwald what happened. At that moment, Orlawn landed. He spoke to Bertchwald the bear, "It's time. You know the burden you must bear."

A sharp pain struck Bertchwald's heart. He cried out with a loud roar that cracked the sky. Down came a strong, thick gray cloud. The cloud passed over them. Lightning exploded from all around the cloud and lit it up. Tears poured out of the cloud and beat the earth directly below. The cloud descended lower to the earth. For many hours, it covered the great forest of the fallen and everyone in it. The rain in the cloud washed them all clean… all but one.

The gray foggy cloud descended on the majors and all the soldiers. It was so thick the army could not even see two feet in front of them. Pashmeira, the witch, saw through the haze, for her stain glass antlers flickered like candlelight around her. It was as if every saint depicted in the church windows hanging upside down from the gallows sacrificing for their beliefs were there with her to guide her path through the antlers.

Pashmeira, the witch, rose from the ground, stood tall, and proclaimed to the army, "Life for life, skin for skin. You will now return to the earth you burned!"

THE BATTLE

The cloud lifted, and the general, the majors, and the soldiers focused their eyes on their surroundings. There, they saw a whole host of bears from all over the forest. Some stood nine feet tall, some stood eleven feet tall, and some stood thirteen feet tall. Every pack of wolves that roamed the forest of the fallen stood next to the bears with fangs awaiting the kill. They remembered their cold winter hunger and were crazed from the famine. Drool dripped from their jaws. They all gathered where the lightning in the sky led them.

Before the general and the majors could see them coming, a parliament of owls led by Orlawn swooped down and gouged out their eyes, all twenty-six eyes. After they plucked the guiding sight from all leaders of the army, the bears and the wolves took out most of the soldiers. Their flesh ripped to shreds by claws and their necks torn open by wild teeth. Brute force pulled apart their limbs. This army burned their sacred land, and a price needed to be paid.

One of Warlawrn's blue eyes turned black, and seeing hell, he was ready to attack. He chased some soldiers up a hill and took down two soldiers at a time. His she-wolf did the same. Other wolves worked in packs and surrounded soldiers before attacking, dodging spears as they circled. One soldier kicked Warlawrn in the side, and he yelped in pain. The powerful kick rolled Warlawrn into another soldier, and they both tumbled off the side of the cliff. Bouncing off the side of the cliff on their way down, Warlawrn stayed tangled up with the soldier. The moment Warlawrn and the soldier hit the ground below, Warlawrn lunged back at him in a flash and bit into the soldier's side, settling the score. The soldier cried out in agony, and Warlawrn bit again, ripping more flesh off as he did. Warlawrn left that soldier to die and climbed back up the cliff, joining the rest of the battle.

The general and majors, without their sight, still tried to fight. Their swords were drawn, and they tried to stab at the animals they heard around them. Warlawrn bit the general's hand, and he dropped his sword. Pashmeira picked up the sword and stabbed the general with it. The sword cut through the general's belly, and he fell to his knees. Warlawrn bit into his jugular, creating a hole in his throat that ended his life. Pashmeira touched her spring garment to him, and the general's body burst into flames and turned to ash, for the light did not cover him.

The bears charged with a strength no match for the soldiers. Sharp black bear's claws sliced and diced the soldiers. Bertchwald charged a troop of four soldiers and knocked three of them down. Once down on the ground, Orlawn gouged their eyes out. This went on for a while until the army dwindled into piles of bloody, mangled dead flesh and bones. A few soldiers got away and tried to escape back to the king and his kingdom. The brave soldier grabbed Pashmeira's hand and ran through the river with her. Bertchwald chased after him—charging with a force like thunder!

The soldier stopped running and turned to face Bertchwald, the bear. Courage is what the brave soldier mustered up when he took out his spear. Bertchwald lunged at him, and the soldier held his spear up, jamming it straight into Bertchwald's heart—slicing it in two.

Orlawn swooped down by Pashmeira and told her to run, and she did. Orlawn circled back and gouged out the last of the soldier's eyes, leaving only the brave soldier escaping back to the kingdom to tell the tale of what had happened. As he ran through the forest back to the kingdom, he heard his heartbeat in his ears. His lungs burned as he ran and ran for his life.

There in the river lay Bertchwald, the bear, on his back, with a spear through his chest. He bled out into the river; the river that gave them life. His blood drained out of his body trickling down stream.

Orlawn and Warlawrn saw his Spirit depart from his body. The sky darkened black again, the earth shook, the mountain cracked, the heavens angered, and the sky whaled. The entire forest mourned.

Pashmeira collapsed behind a tree, crying and shivering. Orlawn and Warlawrn went to her. Orlawn landed on her shoulder. Warlawrn sat close beside her, warming her. He comforted her by nuzzling his head against her neck. His hot breath tickled her. The blood on his whiskers smeared on her cheek, and while the blood from their enemies dried onto their skin, fur, and feathers, they sat in deathly silence over what had just happened.

The next morning Pashmeira's hand branch broom helped her dig the graves, and Warlawrn dug with his paws.

Orlawn spoke to her. "We can't stay here. The other half of the army may come back for you. You must go somewhere else."

Pashmeira looked at Orlawn through her watery black eyes and asked, "Where shall I go?"

Orlawn answered, "Open the compass."

Pashmeira took out the gold and copper compass and when she opened it, a rainbow of color flooded out, and a luminous veil of light covered her. Warlawrn looked over her shoulder at it with his sky-blue eyes, the rainbow gleaming on his fur.

Pashmeira said, "The compass light is pointing northeast towards the kingdom."

"We will enter the kingdom." Orlawn extended his wing over Pashmeira's shoulder.

Pashmeira looked at Orlawn in disbelief. "I will die if we step foot in the kingdom."

"Will you?" Orlawn asked.

Warlawrn scratched behind his ear. "I heard the circus is coming to town."

"We'll enter the kingdom after the first red moon of summer," Orlawn said.

Warlawrn leaned his head back, howling into the night, a sound calling out to death and Hades.

After the battle, the bodies were buried, and the stones and rocks told new tales. Half a league of the forest of the fallen burned up from the church fire. This forced many animals further east, closer to the kingdom. It rained for three days and three nights. Raindrops drizzled from the leaves pattering onto the earth, and Pashmeira's antlers faintly flickered indigo embers of a crushed hope. Rain hit her face like cold cruel tears of grief, and the chilly wind pulled her hair, scratching at her neck. "All bodies are subject to earthly death," she whispered to Warlawrn.

They buried Bertchwald in his cave. An enormous boulder rolled in front of the opening of the cave, sealing it. The rain ceased and, by looking up, Pashmeira witnessed a beautiful rainbow arching over Bertchwald's cave. Yellow rays kissed glowing red beams, making a sweet orange harmony. With a gleam of blue light twisting and turning against the yellow, a green streak shot across a cloud covered sky. With a hopeful spirit, Pashmeira remembered a covenant of life.

She finished the spring in the western section of the forest with Bertchwald's family. The hand branch broom stayed watchful for the other half of the king's army and so did Orlawn. They moved Bertchwald's family to a new cave hidden from plain sight. Pashmeira helped Bertchwald's lady bear to teach the cubs the ways of the forest and helped catch salmon for them at the riverbank upstream; her broom constantly keeping a lookout. She made them all honey cakes to feed their grief and played games with them in the flower fields. Catching a butterfly on your nose awarded you an extra chunk of honeycomb. The cubs delighted themselves in this game in the summer sunshine. They played another game with her blue marble, and the cub that could flick it the farthest won an extra piece of salmon. Pashmeira's antlers shimmered in a warm white light, and that light shined on the marble, making the tangerine swirl twist and turn the cobalt blue marble around. She watched the cubs with the marble and chanted:

"With a royal marble, we will play
under the sun all day.
From eternal death, we are free
by the King's decree.
We will have life
from a sword that cuts like a knife."

The King's Summer Circus

THE KING

King Karlonious Kurlbach was the king, and oh what an evil king he was!

His kingdom reigned glorious,

his army fought victorious,

his victory song rang out rapturous,

his people were forced to be laborious,

and the criminals he executed were notorious.

At the top of a magnificent hill stood his castle

that was designed to bedazzle.

'Twas a hassle

to get to the castle.

You had to cross the moat,

and couldn't do that by boat,

or the alligators would bite at your throat.

The lanterns kept the castle a glow,

and in the winter, it was a safe shelter from the snow.

The king married many wives.

He had one hundred and seventy-five.

He kept them alive,

as long as they didn't contrive

any plans behind his back,

or with the sex appeal lack.

His children were many,

and the mouths to feed were plenty.

He loved them all,

big and small.

If their names he forgot,

he just called them 'little tot'.

Summer was King Kurlbach's favorite season,

and for this reason,

he hosted a circus,

and for fun, was its purpose.

In the tent swung a trapeze artist,

without a harness.

Elephants imported from a far-off land,

while the clowns performed sleight of hand.

Rings of fire held out for the tigers to jump,

while the mighty lion commanded to sit on a stump.

The tamer fearlessly whipped him into submission.

That was his mission.

The bearded lady,

oh, how her facial hair kept her chest shady.

The jugglers kept their balls in the air,

while the man on stilts stood the tallest at the fair.

Eventually, all this fun had to come to an end,

because of the witch, the king had to tend.

He hated evil, and he hated witchcraft.

At her silly spells, he laughed.

He believed her wicked spells

would send her to hell.

After the first time, he left her for dead,

he told her if she stepped foot in his kingdom again, he'd cut off her head.

THE SUMMER SOLSTICE BEGINS

hile Pashmeira helped take care of Bertchwald's family, the king found out he'd lost half his army. "My lord, the animals attacked. There were bears and wolves everywhere. I killed a bear and scarcely escaped with my life. The owls and their talons—they tore out the eyes!" The brave soldier informed the king of the battle in the forest of the fallen.

Barely able to believe the news, the king asked, "Tell me, brave soldier, when you saw the witch, what was she wearing?"

"A dress the bright color of the poppy flowers in the field," the soldier replied.

This intrigued the king, for he knew that was not the garment she wore when his hand caught fire. Looking at the scar on his palm and remembering their encounter, he wondered if the poppy-colored garment could also ignite flames.

The king was a master at the art of war and had never lost a battle before. In his disbelief of his loss, his fear cowardly hid behind his anger. He burned with it, feeling alive. His veins pumped with hatred for the witch—she'd made a fool of him! But what good would it do to send the other half of his army out just to be slaughtered and leave him with no protection? What a foolish strategy that would be. The witch was as powerful as he first suspected. He sent a few soldiers and their horses out across the kingdom bridge onto the dark windy path to keep guard perchance Pashmeira, the witch, tried to enter his kingdom.

In the meantime, he decided his summer circus would still take place, and his half remaining army would recruit and train more soldiers from the neighboring towns. In fact, he would double the size of his previous army, increasing it to the size of two armies. When the circus came to an end, he would keep one army guarding his kingdom, and he would send a full legion army out for her. Surely, she was no match for an entire army.

Dawn broke the next morning, entering the warm summer solstice. The breezy spring season sweltered into summer, and the hot days made Pashmeira decide to fashion a summer garment for herself. She wanted to bathe in the river again before she did. Descending the mountain by herself, she enjoyed the solitude while she strolled along, contemplating everything the last three seasons brought. She knew what waited ahead for her, but for the moment she breathed in her God of earth.

Arriving at the bottom of the mountain, where trees and mountains encompassed the oval river, she looked out at the green abundant land, removed her poppy-colored garment, and set it on a rock. The rock knew why the garment was stained with the blood of many soldiers and knew she would never wear it again. She stood at the water's edge, watching the fish swim around. The water was so clear she could see the rocks at the bottom of the river. She dipped her feet in the sky-blue water. If one witnessed her do this, one would have said her feet walked across the top of the water. It was in her craft to pull an illusion.

The rocks by the river's shore told her tales, and the water in the river held the memory of lovers standing at the cleft of the river, swimming together and holding hands under the waterfall. The water, cool on her feet, felt refreshing. She waded further in and swam over to a waterfall that fed the oval river at the edge of one mountain.

Once on the other side, Pashmeira gathered up some pine needles, soaking them in river water in a hollowed-out branch. She made an oily soap with them and rubbed it on her body to get clean. She took off her antlers and set them on a rock in the sun. As she washed her long fiery hair, the antlers glimmered with the secrets of forbidden fruit, lovers from the garden of Eden shining all around.

She stood under the waterfall, letting the water wash over her. The waterfall was fed by the same river Bertchwald gave his life in. As the stream of water cleansed her, she wondered if there were still remnants of his blood in the river. When she finished washing, she felt whole and clean again. She looked out at the oval river, and the mountains reflected in the glistening crystal blue water were an upside-down mirror image of what sat on the land.

She stepped out from under the waterfall and looked around at the riverland surrounding her. Ringing out her wet hair, she ran her fingers through it. She gathered green leaves, palm fronds, and vines for her summer garment, picking golden sunflowers glowing in a sunny field. She wove vines around her body, fashioning a skirt, attaching palm fronds. For the upper part of her body, she wound vines around herself and wove leaves and sunflowers into them, covering her bosom. That hot sunny day, she fashioned quite an alluring summer sunflower dress.

A rustling sound came from the bushes around. Seeing black fur and blue eyes, she knew Warlawrn hid there, watching. She laid down on a large rock in the sun to get her hair dry. The bushes rustled again. Pashmeira felt his spirit. She opened her eyes and saw Warlawrn standing on the rock next to her. She smiled and petted him.

"How did you know I was here?" Pashmeira asked.

"I smelled you." Warlawrn laid down in the sun next to Pashmeira, and they napped.

When they woke later from a hoot, Pashmeira looked at her antlers sitting on the rock and saw they cast a rainbow streak up into a tall pine tree. Her eyes followed the arched path of iridescent colored light to see Orlawn perched in that pine tree nestled on a branch. It was as if the wisdom of life formed a prism of light around him. She stood under the shade of the tree and waved hello to him. He gave a melancholy hoot.

He flew down from the tree and dropped the scroll into Pashmeira's hand, and with his talons, he tied the back of her summer garment together for her, careful not to remove any of the golden sunflowers. "There will be a red moon tonight," he said.

Pashmeira fluffed her hair and tied her antlers back on top of her head. A whole host of saints and angels danced inside them. She added some sunflowers to her long flame-like hair around her head where the antlers sat.

Her hand branch broom flew to her, landing in front of them. It grabbed the patina covered compass to carry it for her. She placed the handle of the broom through the hollow of the scroll she'd written in the old, abandoned church. They would journey east through the forest of the fallen before going north towards the kingdom. They ventured carefully out into the summer sun, for summer is the season of heat, a heat burning so hot and bright it could ignite a fire of hell even at night.

Summer Celebration

Meanwhile, the circus arrived in the kingdom ruled by King Kurlbach. Down in the valley of the kingdom, they erected huge colorful striped tents with stakes hammered into the ground and ropes strung up to lift them into position. Flags with the king's red and blue emblem flew high above the big top. He'd ordered the finest seamstress in the kingdom to make him a new royal robe of the finest red and blue silk. Those being his colors; red for the blood of his enemies and blue for the color of the sky that covered his kingdom.

The seamstress fashioned a leather belt to go with his robe. "It makes your waist look lean and your shoulders muscular," the alluring seamstress said in a come-hither voice. "I name all the finest garments I make, and this one is called the 'robe of mercy' because you are so merciful, my lord!"

While the seamstress no longer possessed her virginity, and therefore could not be one of the king's wives, this certainly did not stop King Kurlbach from partaking in the seamstress's beauty. This was, after all, his right as a king. The king was so pleased by her; he asked her to make new clothing for all his wives and children, all at the taxpayers' expense, of course.

The best pastry chefs in the kingdom prepared sweet treats and candies for everyone; towers of them. They roasted pigs in pits. Summer fruits were gathered, and fresh breads baked for the royal feast. The wine and ale flowed freely. However, the extra circus folk caused a bit of a food shortage in the kingdom. King Kurlbach ordered the circus workers and animals only be fed the leftovers after the chosen people ate first; the moneychangers, barristers, medicine men, and rope-makers all receiving preferential treatment.

The king's newly enforced army marched around, guarding the circus grounds, keeping order, and making sure no unwanted lowly townspeople entered. Only the chosen could enjoy this circus.

They built booths with games for the children. The jugglers juggled balls. One ball, two balls, three balls going round and round and round in the air. A man on the unicycle rolled through the circus grounds, wobbling as he hit rocks. The big wheel kept turning and turning. The strong man lifted iron high above his head like no other. Another man slid into a cannon and blasted out of it, to the spectators' delight. The lion tamer whipped his ferocious hungry lions into submission. The tightrope walker carefully maneuvered across the line with grace and ease. Men swallowed swords and breathed fire. They threw knives, hardly missing their target. Silly clowns with pointed hats, painted faces, frilly collars, and puffy pants danced around, playing with the children and entertaining them. Joyful pipe organ music played, and they pulled the children around on horse and carriage rides.

The elephants were watered down before the parade began. One elephant blew a horn-like noise out of his huge trunk to signify the start of the circus. Young ladies in jeweled costumes rode on the elephants' backs. White horses with braided manes pranced about merrily. Two-humped camels were trained to give rides to the king's children. The bearded lady grew out her beard—two feet long. The extra lions and tigers stayed captive in cages for everyone to gawk at until it was time for the tigers to jump through rings of fire and the lions to perform on command. Monkeys swung from ropes and poles. Trained bears twirled around with hats on their heads and fluffy skirts around their huge waists, entertaining the audience. Acrobats and contortionists twisted and rotated their bodies around, leaping from place to place at the royal feast while the man on stilts followed sky high behind them; striped pants flowing in the summer breeze.

The circus festival would go for three days straight. After nightfall, the children were told to leave and taken back to the concubine castle, and the dark circus festivities began. As a form of punishment, King Kurlbach made a few of his disobedient wives perform in the peep shows for the chosen men in his town before they met their death. His wives gathered many coins for their performances, which the king confiscated as his right to do so. After a bit too much ale, the king grabbed the lion tamer's whip and beat some of his wives in front of everyone. They were never to be seen again, but they were easily replaced. The virgins that rode the elephants in the parade would do just nicely for the king that night.

If you stood at the tallest mountain next to the town, you could see down into the valley at the bottom of the kingdom where the circus raged about. Someone could peer down and witness all the goings on from a bird's-eye view.

Soon, Pashmeira would stand there, but for the moment, she took the long way through the forest of the fallen to get to King Kurlbach's mighty kingdom.

The Long Way to the Kingdom

The course of the mighty river flowing through the forest of the fallen ran into a series of narrow canyons and rocky barriers. Pashmeira and Warlawrn walked through these paths carefully, with Orlawn circling high above all day. While making their way through one particularly sharp rocky dark path, they came upon the most beautiful spirit Pashmeira ever saw.

The spirit asked, "Behold, I am an angel of the light, and I must know what is your purpose here?" A halo appeared around his head, and his face looked as pure as a snowcapped mountain.

"We are trying to enter the kingdom," Pashmeira answered.

"It is my mission to keep you from the kingdom, for it is too dangerous," the spirit replied, standing in front of a gate leading into the east section of the forest.

Pashmeira spoke, "You will not keep us out."

"You are no match for me," the spirit with the angel's face proclaimed.

Pashmeira, pointing to the wolf, said, "No, but he is."

The spirit turned to the wolf and asked, "Who is this you speak of?"

Orlawn flew down, landing on Pashmeira's shoulder. Orlawn spoke, "He is the wolf Warlawrn, and he has the true Spirit of the forest in him, as do I."

The spirit knew this to be truth and stepped aside letting them pass through the gate, but the beautiful spirit gave them another warning, "If you enter the kingdom, you will not be able to return, and you may lose your life as you know it."

"To die is to gain." Pashmeira stated.

Once through the gate, they continued to head east and made their way through a section of the forest by the old, abandoned church that was badly burned by the king's army. Pashmeira stood near the place where the old, abandoned church once was, now black and desolate. The stones remained in a pile of rubble, and the pews, roof and doors were burned to ashes. The numbered headstones in the graveyard behind the church still rested on their grave mounds. A smokey purple fog rose, swirling around the graveyard. Through the haze, she spotted the light from an angel sitting on a headstone; her wings were burned, and her head was downcast. When the angel looked at Pashmeira, she saw a demon's boney hand grab the angel. Rising from behind the grave mound, the demon wrestled the angel down into it. Pashmeira thought about the spiritual battle going on all around her and shivered, turning away from the grave-yard. Not even she dared to walk through it.

Moving further away, she found a fragment of her autumn garment lying on the ground.

Orlawn landed next to her and said, "You will need this piece of your past for the future."

She picked up the scrap of fabric and tucked it into her summer garment. Looking at the charred ground made her heart ache. Pashmeira bent down and picked up some of the dirt, rubbing it on herself, putting a mark on her throat with the dirty ash.

She saw a war-torn spirit standing by a burned tree stump that once stood as a mighty oak. Pashmeira moved towards the spirit, and in an instant, the spirit disappeared behind a fog of purple smoke. Pashmeira kneeled by the tree stump. There, on the ground by the tree stump, she saw the skeleton of a mouse. Monstros didn't make it out of the forest fire in time. Her black eyes watered.

She rested her hand on the tree stump, saying a magic prayer. The tree began growing back. It resurrected, growing tall and strong again, and its branches reached out into the forest air and sprouted leaves. The trunk turned to gold, and the leaves turned to silver.

She said, "We'll build the forest again upon this mighty oak." Birds from all around flew to it and built their nests. Pashmeira dug a tiny grave next to the gold and silver tree, giving Monstros a proper burial.

Pashmeira, Warlawrn and Orlawn traveled on, and when nightfall was near, they got to a lush section of the forest. A weary Warlawrn said, "Let's sleep here."

"Yes, but first we must eat." Pashmeira found a pear tree heavily laden with fruit and plucked a large measure of them. Orlawn flew to the river and, with his sharp talons, plucked out two fish and flew them back to Pashmeira. She gathered a bundle of wood while Orlawn flew back to the river and got two more fish, one in each talon.

She found two knotted sticks. While rubbing them together to start a fire, Pashmeira recited her witch's chant:

"Friction, friction, smoke, and fire,
Feel the heat burning your feet.
Raising up from the ground
raging flames consuming the earth abound
bringing you down, down
into the depths of hell.
For this reason, we cast a spell

**to ignite the power
at the witching hour.
In us is a sword bearing spirit.
It's calling.
Do you hear it?"**

She held the burning stick to the pile of logs and stoked the fire. Her hand branch broom swept up a pile of leaves for their bed for the night. Pashmeira cooked the four fish on sticks over the fire. They sat around the crackling flames in the dark summer night under the big red moon, eating fruit and fish—two for Warlawrn, one for Pashmeira, and one for Orlawn.

As Warlawrn rested by the fire next to Pashmeira, he queried of her, "Will you tell me the story of the first time you met the king?"

Pashmeira looked at Orlawn, and Orlawn nodded consent.

The Story of When the King Met Pashmeira

Pashmeira looked up at the red moon glowing in the forest's night sky. Fireflies buzzed, flickering all around them in the warm summer night air. The little glimmers of light circled the trees surrounding them. Pashmeira knew it wouldn't be long before she saw the king again. Shuddering, she remembered back to the first time she met the king. She stared into the fire they were gathered around, her eyes black as coal from the memory. Orlawn kept watch on her, and Warlawrn snuggled up against her. The stars in the sky sparkled next to the glowing red moon, the fire crackling.

Pashmeira began her story. "Many years ago, when I was a young girl, right after King Kurlbach and his victorious army force-fully took reign over our land, he demanded all the townspeople pay a high tax. My mother owned an apothecary shop in the mid-dle of town. She brewed many medicines that healed all kinds of ailments in the body. She made medicine that healed the mind too. While many townspeople came to us for healing, her shop did not earn much money. Most sick people couldn't afford to pay for the medicines she gave them. Therefore, she could not afford to pay the tax the king demanded.

"He ordered her to be executed and believed her shop to be full of evil. He proclaimed her to be a witch and sentenced her to be burned. Before the king's soldiers seized her and took her to the king, she gave me her autumn garment. She told me it possessed special powers, but she did not tell me what they were. My mother told me if I were ever to appear before the king, to wear the garment, and she put her compass in the pocket of the garment. She said to always follow the light."

The fire popped and embers burst into the sky. Warlawrn asked, "Did the king execute your mother?"

Pashmeira answered, "Yes, but first he commanded she be brought before him. She was quite beautiful, and he wanted to see her. She was not a virgin and therefore could not be one of his wives. He said that he knew her daughter was also very beautiful. He told her if she gave her daughter over to be married to the king, he would accept that as payment for her tax. My mother believed the king to be evil and said no to him. No one ever dared say no to the king. Saying no to the king meant death. He ordered she be executed, but not before he lay with her first. The townspeople said when they chopped off her head and it hit the ground, the earth shook. When the soldiers burned her body, the townspeople said you could hear the angels and demons screaming."

Warlawrn asked, "What happened next?"

Pashmeira breathed deeply. "The townspeople warned me the king's soldiers were coming to bring me to him. I put on the autumn garment and went before the king. He's a snide, snarly little man, and his mouth watered over me. He said I would be one of his wives. In his excitement, he said to me, 'I leave to you the honor of setting the time when you will lay with me.' I told him, 'This will not happen.', and he burned with anger so strong his face turned bright red. He ordered his guards to have me brought to his chambers first before executing me, but when they approached me and grabbed my arms, they exploded into flames. The king couldn't believe his eyes. He took off his leather belt and began beating me across the face with it."

"You don't have a mark on you," Warlawrn said.

"Oh, but I do. You just can't see them because they are on the inside and in my mind."

Warlawrn asked, "How did you escape the king?"

The witch replied, "I ran out of the castle as fast as I could. The king chased after me because he was so angry. I ran over the bridge all the way to the edge of the forest of the fallen. When I entered the forest, he caught up to me. The second I stepped into the forest; a spiritual battle ensued. Angels and demons rose and descended from everywhere, floods of angels and legions of demons—evil, wicked ones! I could see them all, but the king could not. They stood twice the size of us. Some were bright, and some were dark. Some were male, and some were female. They fought among themselves all around the king and me. I stood trembling with fear and the king still held his belt, beating me viciously as I tried to escape him. I could taste blood in my mouth. The king grabbed my arm, and when he touched my garment, his hand caught on fire. He screamed, and I saw a spirit drag him away. There was fire and pain, and there was wind and rain. It rained so hard I could barely see in front of me. The forest cried, for the wind was wicked."

Warlawrn asked, "Was it an angel or a demon that dragged the king away?"

Pashmeira answered, "I do not know. Sometimes they appear the same. I could not discern that time. The king beat me nearly to death. I lay on the ground aching in agony for a day or two or maybe three. I felt an angel's wing under my head. I cried and cried tears of grief. Then a spirit came along and lifted me off the ground. Lovely she was, with golden wings that span eight feet wide. She said, 'Stand and live, my child, and take cover, for you are in the eye of the storm now.' But it was no longer raining. She helped me up off the ground and walked me further into the forest to the abandoned church. She cleaned my wounds and gave me water to drink and disappeared."

Orlawn, perched on a rock by the fire, said, "That's when I met you."

"Yes, after the spirit left, you were waiting for me inside the church with the magic compass that fell out of my pocket when the king beat me."

Orlawn said, "I saw the spiritual battle. It was the worst one I ever saw in this forest. I wanted to help you. I have watched over you ever since."

Warlawrn's fur rubbed against Pashmeira's leg, and he stayed right by her side. He asked, "Why does the king believe you are evil?"

Pashmeira stoked the fire. "Who is the better one? The good person who does evil, or the evil person who does good?"

"Kurlbach is the father of lies! He is not our Father with the hallowed name." Orlawn's wings fluttered with disdain.

"If you are not the lies the king tells everyone you are, who then are you?" Warlawrn asked.

Pashmeira pet Warlawrn. "I am a believer. I believe in the God of this earth, for the earth is good. I do not believe in the god the king created—the god the king made himself into."

Warlawrn rested his head on Pashmeira's leg. "Why does the king hate you? Because you would not lay with him? Because you burned his hand instead?"

"My mother used to say every king is a slave to his power," Pashmeira answered.

Warlawrn looked at Pashmeira through his vivid blue eyes glowing in the night and said, "Perhaps we should not go to the kingdom. Perhaps it is too dangerous."

A spirit mimicking Pashmeira's voice whispered, "The king promised to kill me the next time he saw me. The compass pointed towards the kingdom, but the compass is wrong, for only death awaits us in the kingdom."

The three of them sat around the fire. The truth that led them stepped back, and the fear of death closed in on them. Light and the dark swirled around and around each other that night, like the serpent through the apple.

The Triune Potion

ashmeira and Warlawrn fell into a deep sleep next to each other on the pile of leaves. Orlawn kept watch for hours, perched on a large rock next to them. His hoot called out in the night to his parliament, and their hoots came back full of warning.

Warlawrn's pack ran through the night, howling and hunting without him. The fire dwindled down to just embers glowing in the dark. When Pashmeira shivered in the night, Orlawn moved next to her, covering her with his wing. Orlawn closed his eyes and fell asleep, too.

In the dark hours of the morning, just before dawn, Pashmeira awoke to the sound of rustling in the bushes and shrubs surrounding them. She sat up. It was quiet again. A bright morning star shined high above them. She heard the rustling again, followed by the crack of a stick. Warlawrn and Orlawn awoke to this noise. The rustling got closer and closer. Warlawrn growled. Orlawn sharpened his talons on the rock.

Like the sound of thunder, they heard a bear growl. Just then, Bertchwald appeared to them, startling all. He stood eleven feet tall on his hind legs and proclaimed, "Behold! I am alive, my friends!"

Pashmeira, frightened and shaking, said, "But we buried you the day you died!"

Warlawrn said, "And you were not easy to move, what with all the honey cakes you ate. The other bears had to help us drag you back into your cave. We rolled a stone in front of it and sealed it."

Orlawn stayed silent.

Pashmeira asked, "What metamorphosis is this? That you would live after you die?"

Bertchwald spoke, "I am alive. Our creator brought me back from the dead. He has sent me here to speak to you. Why do you cower all night at the thought of entering the kingdom?"

Pashmeira answered, "Certainly the king will kill me if he sees me."

Bertchwald spoke again, "Either you go to the King, or the King comes to you, but you will stand face to face and bow your knee. Do you want to run from him all your days here on earth while the king hunts you like a dog and burns our forest and pillages the land?"

Pashmeira shook her head. Lacking faith and doubting, she said, "No, but we are just a girl, an owl, and a wolf. We are no match for the king and his army. He knows the artistry of the battle. He paints pictures with the blood of his enemies."

Bertchwald said to her, "If you are to be his crimson portrait, so be it. You'll follow the stream back east and then go around the outside of the dark windy path true north until you get to the bridge to the kingdom. But first you will make a triune potion and drink it before you enter the kingdom. Pull a hair from my chest, clip a nail from Warlawrn's paw, and pluck a feather from Orlawn's wing. Boil these three things in a skull with river water and drink it."

Pashmeira protested, "But I do not have a skull with me."

Bertchwald scratched his big bear belly. "My dear, this is the forest of the fallen. There are skulls everywhere."

Placing the antlers back on her head illuminated Pashmeira's way like sweet morning light in the golden hour, providing a path for her. She did as Bertchwald instructed by pulling a hair from his chest, seeing the scar from where the brave soldier stabbed him with his spear.

Using the edge of the compass, she chipped off part of Warlawrn's toenail. After she did, it grew back instantly.

Plucking a feather from Orlawn's wing and holding it to her ear allowed her to hear the secrets of the forest. She laughed because the words of the King of kings tickled her ears.

She and Warlawrn walked down towards the stream to find a skull. Warlawrn sniffed and sniffed and sniffed until he stopped sniffing and began digging. He dug up a skull from a lost soul. Pashmeira carried the skull to the stream, cleaning it with water. She unearthed some rocks by the river's edge and plugged the holes in the skull with them. The rocks she held witnessed horrible things, like the battle that caused so many numbered graves behind the old abandoned church. When she held an oval-shaped rock in her hand, she could hear the battle for the church—the screams! She saw King Kurlbach give the order for all parishioners to be executed. The rocks told her the parishioners would not abandon their beliefs for the king, hence they were slaughtered for their faith. "We know now, the church was hardly abandoned," she said to Warlawrn.

She filled the skull with water and added the hair, nail, and feather. They went back to where they camped the night before, and she built another fire. She boiled the contents of the skull over it. After she drank it, she looked around and did not see Bertchwald.

"He is gone," Orlawn said.

"Was he ever really here?" Pashmeira asked.

Warlawrn pointed. "Look, here are his paw prints in the mud!"

Pashmeira, Warlawrn and Orlawn looked closely at one of the paw prints sunken into the forest mud. It filled with water, and reflecting in the water, they could see the circus. They saw the image of the king beating another wife. As he shoved her into the cannon, she cried and pleaded. For his amusement—he shot her out of it!

Pashmeira stood, feeling the full life and Spirit of the forest in her. "I'm ready to travel northeast." Her antlers twinkled speckles of red and blue light all around them.

Without delay, they began their journey east, then true north to the Kingdom.

Kingdom Bound

Instead of taking the dark windy path out of the forest of the fallen, Pashmeira, Warlawrn and Orlawn went around the outside, further east, then north. Orlawn said the king issued another summons and placed some of his soldiers by the kingdom bridge leading into the dark windy path to wait for Pashmeira, the witch, in case she tried to leave the forest to enter his kingdom. For this reason, it was too dangerous to take the dark, windy path. 'Twas even more dangerous to go around the outside of the dark windy path, for it was even darker and windier, and the unwanted forces reigned there in legions.

Pashmeira said, "No path out of the forest exists in the outside section of the woods. Rarely, a soul escape from it."

Orlawn replied, "The path will be provided for us."

Pashmeira filled a skull with water, and they began their pilgrimage. They forged across the dark windy path and further into the surrounding outside darker, windier forest. The trees grew so thick together, they couldn't see the sky above them; not even slivers of light. Pashmeira's antlers served as a lamp unto their feet, shining a soft white light around them.

The ground beneath them lay cold, even in summer. There were no birds chirping in the trees, no flowers blooming. There were no bees making honey. Snakes slithered around on the ground crawling on their bellies like they were commanded to since the beginning of time.

Orlawn flew low and slow between the trees, and Warlawrn stayed close to Pashmeira and led the way. They passed a tree with a raven perched on the lowest branch. The raven stayed silent, barely visible in the darkness of black covering black. Pashmeira felt the raven's eyes on her and turned to look at him. The raven spoke, "The crescent moon will smile down on you tonight."

Pashmeira said, "There is not a crescent moon tonight."

"Oh, my child, there will be," the raven crowed.

Orlawn landed on her shoulder, and the raven flew off.

They kept moving carefully around the outside of the dark, windy path. They trekked along until they came to another tree with a tiny door in the trunk. Orlawn said, "This is Ferloin, the frog's house."

"A frog that lives in a tree?" Pashmeira queried.

The door in the tree opened. Ferloin fashioned himself a comfortable chair from tiny twigs. Fireflies flew around him and lit up his home. His tongue quickly shot straight out, and he caught one on the tip, yanking it back into his mouth and swallowing. Ferloin asked them, "Why are you on the outside of the dark, windy path? You don't belong here. Are you going to see Tammarala, the palm reader? She lives in a tent down the way."

Orlawn answered, "The king's soldiers are on the dark, windy path waiting for Pashmeira."

A croaking noise burped from Ferloin's throat, and he said, "Then I can't be seen talking to you, but I will warn you, the crescent moon will frown down on you tonight."

Pashmeira said, "But the raven said the crescent moon will smile down on us tonight."

Ferloin croaked, "The raven lied to you. Now, please close my door and let me be. I don't want any trouble with the king's men. I do not want my home to burn asunder. And as you move through the outside of the dark windy path, please remember, it is still mating season for us frogs—so mind your own business!"

The three of them pressed on through the thickets of trees and marshes of mud. When they stopped to drink some water, they heard a whisper in the air from behind them saying, "Turn back." When they looked around, they saw a dark shadow with red eyes move through the surrounding trees. Warlawrn let out a long, low growl. The shadow disappeared. They moved through another muddy area with a pond in the middle of it.

A continuous croaking, chirping like sound emanated loudly from the pond. Upon a closer look, a giant female frog swam around in the pond with dozens of male frogs jumping at her—and on her. A frog got on a frog that got on a frog that got on a frog that got on a frog that got on a frog that got on a frog, but this wasn't leapfrog they were playing. Long frog legs intertwined, and slimy frog bodies gyrated and pounded at her. In the midst of this mating frenzy, the female frog almost drowned from the male frogs, who were so libidinous that they did not know or care what they were doing to her. This was nature? This couldn't be good.

As the three of them watched this happen, Orlawn said to them, "Let's keep going. This doesn't concern us."

They took heavy step after heavy step through the muddy marsh until Pashmeira felt a sharp bite on her ankle. She screamed in pain. The hand branch broom she held jumped out of her hand, grabbing a black snake so dark he blended into the mud. The broom's hand strangled the snake until its breath left its slithery body. Pashmeira sat down on a rock, crying in pain. Warlawrn attended to her wound and sucked the poison out of the bite. He sucked and spat out the venom quickly. While he did, another snake slithered towards them. Orlawn swooped down and grabbed the snake with his talons, flinging him away from them.

Orlawn landed on Pashmeira's shoulder again and said, "If you can walk, we need to keep moving. We need to get out of here before the unwanted forces awaken."

Warlawrn licked Pashmeira's wound a few more times for good measure, and she stood from the stone she was seated on. They walked again slowly. They climbed up over dark hills, around trees, through bushes and around more trees. Eventually, the air got a little lighter and warmer. They were getting close to the edge of the forest of the fallen.

She asked, "Should we stop at Tammarala's tent?"

Orlawn asked, "Whatever for?"

Answering him, she said, "To tell our fortune, of course."

Orlawn said, "Your future is in the hands of God. 'Twas already written in the stars."

"I must see what is in the cards for me," Pashmeira said.

When they were moving through a thick section of trees, a hand reached out and grabbed Pashmeira. She screamed, and the hand grabbed at her garment. It pulled on the palm fronds, and the hand of her broom swatted it away. Another hand of unwanted force grabbed for the scrap of the autumn garment she had tucked into the side of her summer garment. Orlawn spread his wings wide and flew towards the unwanted spirit force. He hit it with his talons as hard as he could. The spirit disappeared, and some of Orlawn's feathers scattered into the air. Pashmeira and Warlawrn ran the rest of the distance to Tammarala's tent. Their muddy feet and paws climbed uphill. Warlawrn led the way, and Orlawn brought up the back, making sure nothing and no one got to Pashmeira.

Tammarala's tent hung like a heavy cloak of mysticism from a dead, black prickly tree with dim candlelight glowing from a loose seam in the tapestry. A painted sign harboring the image of a hand with one eye on the palm hung from a noose tied to a branch. A shrill, crying wind blew it back and forth.

"I do not advise this," Orlawn said. "But if you insist, so be it."

Pashmeira hurried towards the tent with Warlawrn at her side.

Pashmeira called out to Tammarala. She'd seen her once before when Pashmeira was a young girl, but when King Kurlbach took reign, he banished the dark arts. Tammarala escaped to the forest of the fallen before he could burn her.

Upon hearing Pashmeira's voice, Tammarala poked her head out of the tent, her eyes never more than gray soot. Tangled hair stuck out from the scarf wrapped around her head. Her teeth biting like brown kernels of corn. Tammarala looked at Orlawn, asking, "What is he doing here?"

Pashmeira pleaded, "Please, I must have a reading."

Tammarala spoke, "Alright, but he stays out."

Orlawn agreed, and Warlawrn entered the tent with Pashmeira and sat at her feet. Her broom guarded the outside of the tent.

"I already read your palm when you were a child. You must want the cards," Tammarala said, shuffling the tarot deck.

Pashmeira nodded.

Long boney fingers with dirty nails dealt three cards down. Turning them face up, with a voice as old as ninety years, she wheezed, "The moon, the talisman, and the fire eyes."

Pashmeira stared at the card with a full moon, and an owl perched in front of the moon. She asked, "What does this mean?"

The palm reader said, "The first card represents your past. The moon card shows your father has been watching over you."

"I do not have a father," Pashmeira protested.

"Oh, but you do, my dear. You just can't see him," Tammarala said. "The second card... the talisman... you have something on you with an ornate carving on it, or you would not have drawn this card."

"The compass," Warlawrn said, looking at Pashmeira.

Tammarala read on, "The second card represents the present time. Drawing the talisman card means you hold something of great value."

"What are the fire eyes? What does that mean?" Pashmeira asked.

"The third card represents the future." Tammarala stared at the card with the image of the fiery eyes on it, and her eyes glowed. "The fire eyes bring a power so awesome your mind can't fathom it—a power that can destroy! They bring a fire on earth!"

Pashmeira gasped, "The King!"

Warlawrn urged, "We must go now."

Without haste, they traveled on and arrived at the edge of the forest, seeing a bit of late afternoon light gleaming through the trees. They emerged out of the path they forged, and they stood atop a tall mountain by the kingdom bridge overlooking the valley of King Kurlbach's raging circus. They stared in horror and disbelief at what they saw.

From the mountain they stood on, a dark shadow cast over the circus down in the valley below... a circus of debauchery.

The Three-Ring Circus

own in the valley below them, dozens of the wives were fran-
tically escorting their children out of the circus and to their
separate concubine castle for safety. At this circus, when day
turned to night, it could give such a fright.

Several of the king's wives weren't so lucky as to make it back to
the family castle. Some hungry lions roamed back and forth, waiting
in the arena. At the king's command, they led a half dozen of his wives
who could not bear children into the arena, never to be seen again.

Other wives, with chains around their hands and feet, were led
into the circus tent. The balls and chains trailed behind them like a
death sentence. Pashmeira looked on in horror and asked Orlawn,
"What are the goings on in the tent?"

Without a sound, Orlawn glided down into the valley to take
a closer look. Returning from flight, he reported, "To the soldiers,
the frogs be demure."

Pashmeira picked up a stick with misshapen branches appearing like a scythe. She kneeled down to the earth, and in the dirt, she

drew out part of the battle strategy. The grim stick reaped a plan of death. When she stopped drawing on the land, the hand branch broom finished the drawing for them; the full plan sketched out on the ground before them.

The view down into the valley gave them eyes to see the total lay of the land. Their plan was so simple, Pashmeira feared it would not work. Of the battle strategy, Pashmeira asked, "Must we burn down the bridge leading into the kingdom? We cannot get back out if we do so."

With a fire burning in his chest, Warlawrn replied, "There is no turning back once we enter the Kingdom, and no one escapes out of the kingdom on the bridge once we go to battle. I will take down the soldiers guarding it, and you will start the fire at the appointed time."

Orlawn called for his parliament with commanding hoots through the air.

Warlawrn howled for his pack.

The afternoon sun turned to dusk, and dusk dissolved into a blanket of darkness while they waited.

Orlawn went first.

Orlawn's wings, as reticent as a mute, flew him down into the valley. Precise talons covertly undid the locks on all the circus animal cages. One by one, he unlocked the cages of the lions, tigers, bears, monkeys, elephants, giraffes, horses, and camels. They had deprived the ravenous lions and tigers of food for two days. They wanted flesh ground in their teeth—blood on their tongues! Starving, they roamed the circus grounds. The biggest, mightiest lion went for the lion tamer first, and the sting of the whip, the lion remembered. The arrogant lion tamer grabbed for his stool and tried to push the lion back. But the lion tamer didn't have his whip, for the king had used it to punish some of his wives. The lion's paw jabbed hard across the lion tamer's face. Blood gushed from his cheek, tasting delicious to the lion.

More lions and tigers pounced on those around them. Screams from the chosen townspeople cried out into the air, ensuing a panic, and running for their lives.

Soldiers battled a futile fight with the lions and tigers kicking up clouds of dust, dust which they would return to. While the lions and tigers devoured everyone around them and stood on a hill of bones, Orlawn led the circus bears into the tent, where the soldiers committed all kinds of debauchery on women from the town. He gave them strict orders not to harm the women. Orlawn undid the ropes to the tent, and it collapsed on itself. The bears growled and clawed at the soldiers who terrorized the women. Their knife-like claws ended the pillage. One of the circus monkeys took a key from a slain soldier, unlocking the chains of the wives, setting them free. They ran back to their concubine castle to get out of the chaos.

The horses charged a stampede of all the hooved animals, trampling soldiers and stomping the chosen and the soldiers. Dust clouds blocked their sight; powdered earth was thick and choking their throats. The weight of the horses crushed many soldiers, and camels, zebras and giraffes smartly kicked their hooved feet, knocking in skulls. The elephants crushed heads under their thick legs, like grapes for a blood wine.

A few soldiers seized the king and quickly escorted him back to his castle. Other soldiers stood guard on the drawbridge while they got him to safety. Lightning flashed in the sky behind the tall stone ornate fortress. Thunder cracked and rumbled all around them. The heavens were angry, and the storm was coming. A darkened sky filled with rolling clouds around the moon, making it look like a frowning mouth as they covered part of it.

The royal stone castle towered high above the valley circus; chaos ensuing below. Orlawn and his parliament flew low to the ground, gouging out eyeballs that rolled along the drawbridge to the king's castle.

Warlawrn snuck up behind the two soldiers sitting on their horses, guarding the bridge to the kingdom. He pounced on the first, knocking him off his white horse. With the soldier lying on his back, Warlawrn attacked, killing the first soldier in seconds. The second soldier dismounted his red horse and drew his sword. Warlawrn jumped up and bit the second soldier's hand, making him drop his sword. He tore his hand off, going for his jugular quickly after that. Warlawrn and the red horse raced down the bridge to the kingdom for war, while the white horse ran for freedom into the forest of the fallen. Like a bolt of light, the white horse disappeared out of sight under the moonlight to warn the forest animals of the fire fright that would soon ignite. The wolves appeared out of the darkness and followed Warlawrn across the bridge.

Next to the dead soldiers lying upon the bridge to the kingdom, Pashmeira rubbed two sticks together chanting:

"Into the black night lightning crack.
You'll feel the wolves biting at your back."

Holding the burning sticks to the wooden bridge connecting the kingdom to the forest of the fallen, Pashmeira lit it on fire. She crossed the bridge quickly, a fire raging behind her. A firefall of ash drifted down into the dark valley below. The crackle and pop of burning wood whistled in her ears. Smoke invaded her nostrils, and her honey-colored eyes danced with fire turning black. Entering the kingdom for the first time since her exile, she didn't dare look back at the pillar of flames behind her. Storm clouds presented themselves, angry and ready to cry. Pashmeira traveled up towards the king's castle.

Out of the lightning, thunder rumbled and Warlawrn burst onto the castle drawbridge ahead of Pashmeira. One of his sky-blue eyes turned black as night. Running with his pack, they began their attack, and when those wolves set their eyes on you—a terror would ensue.

Attacking the sightless soldiers guarding the castle, Pashmeira's hand branch broom of destruction grabbed spears out of their hands, stabbing them with their own weapons, sweeping them to their death. Warlawrn knocked soldiers off the drawbridge to the castle, one by one, biting at their ankles. His she-wolf got under their legs, bucking them off the drawbridge. They dived into the moat below, only to be food for the alligators. Other soldiers' faces were bitten at with a force they could not recover from. Limbs were torn from their bodies and devoured by the wolves.

Amidst all this pandemonium, Pashmeira marched down the middle of the drawbridge. Holding the key to the castle Crueneilious gifted her, she chanted:

"From the King, I will not flee.
To the Kingdom, I have a key.
I walk into the castle
with the demons to rassle.
Under the pale light of the crescent moon,
it will be over soon."

The antlers on top of her head burned as bright as the torch flames lighting up the front of the stone dwelling of the mighty ruler. She unlocked the castle door with the key and entered, remembering what the king promised to do to her if he saw her again.

She looked up at the ceiling forty-five feet above her. The candelabra dripped hot wax down the shaft of the candles and onto the iron base. The light glowed softly in the dark castle. An empty throne sat twenty-five feet in front of her, resting on higher ground than the ground her dirty feet stood upon. The stones on the walls pleaded with her, and she grieved their words.

Walking up to the brave soldier, she said, "I am Pashmeira, the witch. The King summoned me, and I'm here to surrender to Him."

THE SURRENDER

The brave soldier summoned two other soldiers who went to notify the king Pashmeira, the witch had entered the kingdom's castle. Pashmeira stood twenty-five feet in front of the king's throne, waiting for him. The brave soldier guarded her. His spear poked into her back, rubbing against the leafy vines wrapped around her body.

Minutes later, two soldiers appeared out of the darkness of the castle, a tall, muscular soldier on King Kurlbach's right, and an even taller, more muscular soldier on King Kurlbach's left. Footsteps from the king's boots echoed from the regal castle walls; the castle stones silenced by his presence. The king walked closer to Pashmeira and light emanated from her antlers, making the blue silk of his robe glisten in the dark royal court. The smell of death hung in the air, but the knowledge of it being hers or the kings was withheld from Pashmeira.

King Kurlbach seated himself at his stately throne. His royal gold goblet sat at his right hand, filled with the finest wine. Pashmeira humbly bowed her knee before him. The soldiers stood one on each side of the throne. Pashmeira, the witch, spoke to the king, "Your majesty, I am here to surrender to you."

The king gazed at her. He looked upon the sunflowers adorning her chest. This pleased the king, and the palm fronds around her hips intrigued him. Enamored by her splendid apparel, the king spoke to her, "Pashmeira, the witch... I had forgotten all about you. I haven't thought of you in years, but now I remember the day you stood before me for the first time. This dress you wear is not the garment you wore the last time you appeared before me." He sipped his wine. "Do you remember what happened the last time you appeared before me?"

Pashmeira bowed her head, nodding. She replied, "I think of you often, my king. I think how foolish I was to run from you. I wish I had agreed to be one of your wives."

Thinking of his secret cache of treasures for the lovely Pashmeira, the king asked, "What is the price for your body?"

"The price for my life has already been paid," Pashmeira said.

"I did not ask for your life. I asked for your body. You should remember I do not have to ask. I can take whatever I want."

"All the gold and silver cannot buy me."

"You would give your body freely to me?" the king wondered.

Pashmeira smiled and nodded. "I have seen the writing on the wall. I know my fate. I even fashioned a new garment for you of vines and sunflowers. Do you like it?"

The king snarled and inquired, "Does this garment start fires, too?"

Pashmeira stood up and looked at the king, answering, "No, your majesty, but I can remove it if that would make you more comfortable." She smiled.

The king's heart fluttered with excitement. He commanded, "Yes, Pashmeira. Remove the garment you wear, and I will bathe you in milk and honey." The king nodded to the brave soldier guarding her, and he stepped back.

Pashmeira gently began removing the large sunflowers covering her torso and pulling the larger sunflowers from the vines wrapped around her waist. She placed them in a pile on the ground, their scent still fresh in the air. Next, she reached her right hand up to her right breast and slowly plucked the smaller sunflowers from it, exposing it to the king's pleasure. Reaching her left hand up to her left breast, she slowly plucked those sunflowers from it, exposing it to the king's delight. She unwound the remaining vines from her upper body until it was completely bare—the vines of her summer garment on the ground.

Turning around with her back to the king, she pulled off the palm fronds from her bottom. She slowly bent over and set those in the pile, turning back around and facing the king, revealed drool pooling at the edges of his lascivious mouth. The palm frond from her right hip gently floated to the ground, followed by the palm frond from her left hip. The king salivated for the palm frond covering her groin to be stripped off; she let it flutter down to the ground. It withered and turned away from the king. Pashmeira slowly unwound the last vine from her tiny waist, dropping it.

There she stood before the king, no clothing to cover her body. King Kurlbach leered at her, licking his lips. His loins swelled at the sight of her.

The lonely, exiled little caterpillar emerged from her cocoon, and the beautiful butterfly appeared. In awe of her beauty, the king rose. From his mighty throne, the king walked towards Pashmeira, the witch with the royal goblet in hand. He stopped a foot in front of her. Her antlers cast a red hue across his vile face. "My lovely bride to be, commune with me and drink from my cup."

Pashmeira took the cup from him and held it with both hands. Putting it to her lips, she drank the wine.

"Good," he said, taking off his leather belt and holding it in his right hand. With his left hand, he caressed her soft breast. The three soldiers stood and watched, unable to move. The king mockingly asked her, "Without your garment, what do you have to save you, Pashmeira?" With the belt in his dominant hand, the king stepped back and whipped Pashmeira across her stomach with it.

Pashmeira curled back away from him in agony, dropping the empty gold cup on the ground. This was how he got his name, Kurlbach.

He commanded her to turn around, and Pashmeira presented her back to him. Her flaming red hair hung long down her back. He whipped at it in anger over and over, feeling his power. She pleaded with him to stop, but every plea fueled the fire blazing in him. Pashmeira fell down from the pain, her knees burning when they hit the stones. Warm blood oozed from the scrapes, and the stinging in her hands itched. The king commanded her to get up. Fearfully, she dragged her aching body up from the royal ground. She couldn't stand still for the trembling.

"Face me!" he commanded. Pashmeira turned her body around again to face the king. Her black eyes met his, and the stench of death permeated her nostrils. The king spoke, "My brave soldier here told me of the forest battle. He told me of the bear he killed."

"Bertchwald's loyalty to me knew no bounds," Pashmeira replied. "He died to save me." She looked intently at the king, the gold crown on his head shining brightly and fire blazing in his eyes.

The king queried, "Again, I ask you, without your garment, your bear, and your owl, what do you have to save you?"

Pashmeira raised her right hand up in the air. She turned her hand—palm facing her and grabbed her right antler. Swiftly cracking it off—she stabbed the piece of jagged glass horn into the left side of King Kurlbach's neck. A gurgling sound came out of his throat, and his eyes bulged. She cranked the piece of horn glass across his throat, slitting it. Blood sprayed out on her naked body. She watched him fall to the floor, his throat gushing blood. His gold crown tumbled off his head, landing on the royal ground next to him. Blood stained the stones beneath him, and they would tell new tales. Pashmeira said to the king's dead body, "You were the plague on this land."

As the two soldiers rushed forth from the throne to seize Pashmeira, the witch, Orlawn, the owl, flew into the castle. Pashmeira turned towards the brave soldier who lunged to capture her. With the jagged fossilized piece of glass antler still in her hand, she stabbed the brave soldier—a strike right through the heart. He froze, lighting up like a rainbow. Pashmeira pulled the jagged glass antler back out of his heart, and he fell to the ground, bleeding out.

While this happened, Orlawn's talons quickly plucked out the eyes of the two soldiers. Warlawrn the wolf entered the castle, fresh from the drawbridge battle and bloody with victory. In one bound, he took down the two tall, muscular soldiers in a blind battle.

Pashmeira bent down over the king's lifeless body and pulled off his robe of mercy. She covered herself in it and took the belt from his dead hand, fastening it around her waist. She picked up the fragment of her autumn garment and, like a pall, she set it on top of the king's corpse, stepping back as flames ignited. She watched the king burn and turn to ashes—the castle stones cheering.

Pashmeira looked at Warlawrn; his eyes were as blue as the sky and hers as warm as sweet honey. Still panting from the battle, he looked upon Pashmeira. With one antler on her head and blood and bruises all over her, he saw how war-torn she really was, and he loved her even more for it. He said, "You are worthy to open the scroll now."

She picked up the scroll, and they walked forth from the castle; the ashes of the king behind them. Orlawn picked up the king's crown with his talons. Pashmeira stood at the entrance of the castle with Warlawrn at her side and saw dead soldiers; bodies all along the drawbridge. She peered out into the valley through the night. The circus was over, bloody bones scattered about, the animals disbursed into the kingdom, and the townspeople hid in fear. Out of that chaos would come a new order.

Her hand branch broom, still inside the castle, swept up King Kurlbach's ashes, pouring them into an urn. The hand of the broom dipped one of its twiggy fingers into the urn and, with his ashes, wrote a message on the castle wall:

It is finished!

The broom carried the urn out of the castle and spread the ashes over the water in the moat. When King Kurlbach's ashes hit the water, it bubbled and hissed, turning the alligators to stone.

Pashmeira closed the door to the castle and unrolled the scroll she'd written to the townspeople of the Kingdom. Holding it up onto the door, she stabbed the broken antler into the top of the scroll, securing it to the door between the wooden planks. Her hand branch broom broke off the other antler and stabbed it into the bottom of the scroll to hold it in place. She walked down the drawbridge, and the clouds moved around the moon, making it look like a crescent smile—looking up at the moon, she smiled back.

The stain glass antlers melted onto the scroll and dripped down the door, solidifying it. The paper shined like a rainbow, illuminating a path of light down the drawbridge. Pashmeira, covered in the King's cloak of mercy and free from exile, entered the Kingdom with Warlawrn and Orlawn to receive what riches it offered. She'd been called out of darkness and into the light. All around them, the colors from the melted glass antlers stained the land and glimmered radiantly. The light shined brightly for every sinner and saint who lived and died to speak the truth in the quest of every believer's freedom, for all eternity.

Orlawn flew over Pashmeira, placing the King's crown of glory on her head. There behind her, the scroll read:

Your King is dead.

We slit his throat.

Kurlbach burned like rubbish

because he lived so sluttish,

and we threw his ashes into the moat.

All his soldiers are gone,

for they, too, did wrong.

The God in heaven who reigns over this earth,

for all His people gave birth

to truth and freedom,

and this Lord will not mislead them.

The king of kings from above

Will give you eternal love.

About the Author

Drew Dunmoore is a California native and enjoys visiting local amusement parks. Drew has worked in the financial services industry for twenty years but has been obsessed with writing for more than forty years. This is Drew's third book.

To check out other books Drew has written, visit the following website:

www.dunmooredisports.com

Readers can reach Drew at ddunmoore@gmail.com

Follow Drew on Instagram: @drewdunmoore